To Ting

Club 27

Best wishes

MARTIN TRACEY

Copyright © 2018 Martin Tracey

Martin Tracey has asserted his right under the Copyright, Designs and Patents Act, 1988 to be the author of this work.

All rights reserved.
No part of this publication may be reproduced, stored in or introduced into a retrieval system, or transmitted, in any form, or by any means (electronic, mechanical, photocopying, recording or otherwise) without the prior written permission of the author in line with publishing guidelines.
If you wish to read this work you are kindly advised to please purchase a copy. Thank you for respecting the hard work of the author.

All characters and names in this publication, other than those clearly in the public domain, are the product of the author's imagination and any resemblance to persons, living, dead or undead is entirely coincidental.

Cover artwork by Ares Jun 2018 based on an original idea by Martin Tracey.

ISBN: 9781983129940

DEDICATION

For all who are said to be members of the 27 Club, with the deepest respect.

And for George Michael, not recognised as a '27' member but a singer, songwriter, musician, philanthropist and inspiration who left this world far too soon.

Also by Martin Tracey

BENEATH THE FLOODLIGHTS
THINGS THEY'LL NEVER SEE

In the Judd Stone Series

MIND GUERRILLA

ACKNOWLEDGEMENTS

Special thanks as ever to my family who allow me the time to flex my literary muscles and to tour the country when my stories take me here, there and everywhere.
Thanks to my social media family and author networks. Your support is truly invaluable.
Thanks once again to cover designer Ares Jun. I still can't comprehend how you manage to transport what's inside my head into reality. Perhaps your powers of perception can even exceed those of William Chamberlain!
Special thanks to Jax and Bex for your incredible unwavering support and in particular for the fresh eyes of Jackie 'Jax' King which were kindly cast over this manuscript.
Thanks to Alisa Keogh who believes this book should have been called *Never 28* - a valiant attempt and your interest in this literary work is noted with appreciation.
And last but by no means least…
Dear reader, thanks as ever for reading my words. Without a reader, there is no story to tell.

CHAPTER 1
THE FOOL

The slap to Judd Stone's left cheek came fast and sharp.

"Brooke, let me explain," offered Judd lamely as he distinctly felt the sting of his soon to be ex-girlfriend's strike.

In truth what could he explain? Judd's words were simply a typical reaction when one is caught with one's pants down. Literally! The harsh reality of the situation was that Brooke already knew what had been going on and for Judd, there was no squirming his way out of anything.

"Allow me to explain it to you instead, Judd?" spat Brooke with an enormous amount of venom. "You've been screwing that 'has-been' over there for the best part of three months."

"Excuse me, do you know who I am?" The voice came from the bottle-blonde whose modesty was shrouded only by a sheet in the hotel's king size bed.

"Yeah, I know who you are and you don't frighten me."

"Well, maybe you should be frightened." The tone was deliberate and menacing but Brooke was far too angry to be fazed.

"It's you who should be frightened, Gia Talia. Not me. You're finally going down."

"Well I was just about to actually, until you interrupted proceedings that is," smiled Gia smugly.

"You disgust me. I won't take your bait, Gia. You'll get yours."

"It was Judd who was about to get his."

Brooke ignored the loaded jibes and turned her attention back to her cheating boyfriend. "What is wrong with you, you freak? Sleeping with a known criminal who has implemented extortion rackets and even orchestrated the deaths of people. What on earth possessed you? You're better than that, or at least I thought you were."

"I'm working undercover," but Judd realised how lame he sounded as the words left his mouth.

"No, you're not. Your taking me for a fool stops right now. She's already awaiting trial and you're telling me that a crime lord, or lady rather, and I use that term very loosely indeed, with her connections doesn't know you're a copper? She's using you more than you are her, you idiot. She thinks that she can manipulate the evidence by manipulating you. She's engineering matters so that her trial will implode."

Judd's only answer was to hang his head in shame. Initially he had been working undercover but of course, Gia knew exactly who she had been sleeping with and it hadn't been a problem for either of them. Opposites attract.

Judd had been one of the main investigating officers in a significant sting involving Birmingham's gangland culture. He had been one of the coppers dangerously playing with the big boys, and girls as it happened: Gia Talia was the notorious head of one of the most sophisticated and dangerous gangster operations north of London and the danger had excited him. She was a feared lady with a terrifying reputation and Brooke had shown tremendous courage in confronting her today. Others before her who had dared to cross the formidable Ms. Talia were now sleeping with the fishes or propping up motorways for less.

Gia had already fathomed Judd's occupation way before her arrest by another officer, but she had been attracted to the unorthodox crime fighter. He wasn't like the other coppers she knew, some of whom she had in her pocket as a necessary evil yet she still loathed them. In fact, she often thought that Judd Stone would fare much better operating on her side of the law rather than on the right side. Boy, she had been expertly persuasive with him on many levels but he had informed her that no matter what she could pull out of the bag he would never willingly walk away from the job.

Judd couldn't help himself in being attracted to Gia. She was older than him but still a looker with a figure that belonged to someone at least twenty years her junior and her reputation coupled with the vast experience in her field demanded his respect for the woman. She generated an aura of danger which only served to heighten her attractiveness and it was in Judd Stone's DNA to play with fire.

But Judd and Gia were never in love. It was Brooke he loved in spite of his relationship with Gia. Gia and Judd simply held a kindred spirit and the sense of danger for both of them fuelled their mutual attraction for one another. Once fate had brought them together the magnetism was just too strong to ignore and inevitably they engaged in a very physical coming together. The sex was undeniably electric but Gia wasn't Brooke, and now it was too late. Judd sadly realised that he had blown it with his wonderful girlfriend.

"How did you find out?" enquired Judd, finally accepting it was useless to try and deny the affair.

"I hired a private detective once I suspected things. Obviously, he was a bloody good one, too wasn't he? Now consider this Judd Stone before you go back to your whore…"

"You're on your last warning you little bitch," snarled Gia.

"Leave her alone, Gia. She's entitled to be upset."

"And don't you forget who you're speaking to either Stone."

"…Do you think Frankie would have been proud of you if she could see you now, Judd?" finished Brooke.

Judd couldn't bring himself to answer her.

"Just remember this, Judd. You have lost the best thing that has happened to you since Frankie's death so I hope your sordid little affair was worth it."

And with those final words, Brooke walked out of the hotel room and out of Judd's life.

But Judd wasn't prepared to let things end there.

In spite of how much he missed her, he didn't chase after Brooke sensing that bird had well and truly flown, but once he had tracked down the Private Investigator who Brooke had hired he had a *conversation* with him in true Judd Stone style and put the interfering meddler in hospital.

Once the PI was able to eat solid food again and could talk to police he pressed charges, and this time Judd Stone could not be saved from dismissal. Not even DSI Ben Francis, a man of unprecedented reasoning who had influenced his peers and prevented previous threats of kicking Judd Stone off the force was able to save him. The assault charge against the PI coupled with the likelihood of compromising the investigation into Gia Talia was enough for DCI Judd Stone to be relieved of his duties. The fact that he beat up the two arresting officers, who he had never liked, had also played an inevitable part in influencing things.

And by now best friend and mentor William Chamberlain had retired from the force so William's calming influence and ability to vouch for his wayward sidekick was no longer in place. In reality, the clock against Judd's career in law enforcement had started ticking the day he and William had parted professional company.

Judd Stone had lost his lovely and loyal girlfriend and also his distinguished and illustrious career as a Detective Chief Inspector.

Basically, Judd Stone was fucked and the only person he could blame was himself.

CHAPTER 2
THE POP STAR

Phoenix Astrid Easter had not long turned twenty-six years old. She possessed stunning beauty, was intelligent beyond her years and had a zest for life which ironically placed her own at risk. Constantly searching for something new she was willing to try almost anything once. And that often included drugs and alcohol.

Like many pop stars before her, Phoenix was well-known by her forename alone. Her parents had settled on the name following the traumatic experience when their newborn baby girl had not been breathing when she initially entered the world. This caused enormous concern amongst the midwives and doctors who rushed around speaking in what seemed like a language all of their own and the distressing minutes that passed seemed to last an eternity. But then something, somehow, seemed to intervene and against all the odds the little girl cried out in that famous voice of hers for the first time. To Earl and Teagan Easter, the name Phoenix made perfect sense to them as their little miracle had seemingly become born-again.

In spite of her career finding her in such tender years, Phoenix was already a winner of a ridiculous amount of BRITS, Grammys and Ivor Novello Awards. With a dedicated and ever-increasing fan base that stretched around the globe, Phoenix possessed a very rare and self-generating talent, but one which could never fully escape the fruits of her heritage.

Earl Easter had been born in Kingston, Jamaica and had been a bass player in a small number of reggae and SKA bands. Teagan Easter nee Malone was born in Dublin, Ireland and played the accordion as a young girl but quickly lost interest in the instrument. Words were Teagan's passion, she could speak eloquently and she secretly loved to write poetry but never had the confidence to do much about her writing talent. She merely viewed her writing as a hobby, but with a stronger sense of purpose, she could have probably achieved so much more.

Earl and Teagan met in their teens at their secondary school in Sparkhill, Birmingham and hit it off straight away. They were of a kindred spirit and soul mates in the truest definition of the term. Earl couldn't resist her bright red hair with their wisps of sandy colour which appeared in a certain light. He also fell in love with her angelic smile. Teagan couldn't resist Earl's sense of humour and ability to laugh in the face of anything. Earl was so laid-back Teagan would often poke her man teasingly to 'check that he hadn't stopped altogether.'

They faced prejudice from all quarters but this only proved to make them a stronger couple with a solid commitment to one another. There were times when they even enjoyed the rebellion against the ingrained narrow-mindedness of the majority and through their flaunting love metaphorically stuck up two fingers to the bigoted establishment.

Phoenix was their only child and she was born in the Easter's first home in Sparkhill before moving up the road to Moseley when Earl got promoted from bus driver to

Inspector on the West Midlands bus network. At that time Phoenix was seven years old.

Moseley was the perfect place for a surefire talent like Phoenix Easter to grow up in. The rich cultural tapestry that Moseley had to offer could ensure that her creative senses were never suppressed but instead always evolving and sharpened. Moseley possessed considerable diversity, a multitude of nationalities and a genuine Bohemian ambience.

In Moseley, there were the rich and not so rich. There were professionals, working-class heroes and students. There was a variety of traditional pubs and swanky bars, yet a cluster of harmless down and outs could always be spotted sinking cheap wine and lager on the central benches. There were cafes offering filtered coffee and home-made cakes that were then contrasted by the fine dining restaurants of the world. There was an assortment of approaches to fashion, including hippies, mods, rockers, indies, wearers of various hats, clubbers and those that followed no particular fashion at all, instead choosing to creatively reinvent second-hand clothes with additions of badges or alternative scraps of brightly coloured material.

And importantly, Moseley has always possessed a healthy approach to embracing different types of music, literature and art ensuring that its population is one of rich innovation and imagination.

But none more so than Phoenix Astrid Easter.

CHAPTER 3
THE PRISONER

Judd Stone had taken just two mouthfuls of his dinner when he saw the tray of food overturn onto the floor.

"It's ok, I wasn't hungry anyway."

A hand slammed down on the dining table as bodies of inmates began to swarm around the scene edging for the best view and sensing a fight was about to take place.

"The face with its squashed nose and craggy features moved closer to the seated Judd. "Why don't you finish your meal by licking it off the floor, Pig? After all, that's what pigs do, isn't it? Eat their food off the floor."

The aggressor known as Freeek, a nickname since his teens apparently, and one that suited the huge and ugly man for sure, moved his face away from Judd as his hangers-on laughed out loud.

Judd refused to look at the horrible beast. His arms remained folded and he looked ahead as he spoke. "I don't want any trouble?"

"Well, that's just too bad, Pig. Because you've got it."

"Look. I just want to keep my head down and do my time. I'm no threat to you in here."

Judd had been handed a six months custodial sentence in an experimental super-prison being piloted somewhere on the continent following a unique deal with European authorities. Banged-up Brits still contributed heavily to the super-prison population. Judd's sentence was for Actual Bodily Harm against the Private Investigator. It could have been much worse; the charge was borderline Grievous Bodily Harm which would have attracted more time behind bars. On sentencing, the Judge had stated that a custodial sentence was the only option as Detective Chief Inspector Judd Stone had failed in his duty to protect the public and had ironically inflicted a dangerous assault on a member of that public who should have been expected to be able to view him as a symbol of trust and decency. The judge added that DCI Judd Stone had seriously let down his colleagues and brought the Police Force into disrepute. As it turned out the two coppers who had also felt Judd's wrath chose not to press charges, which was something, they were just happy that a loose cannon like Judd Stone was off the force.

Freeek slammed the table once more. "That's right you are no threat to me in here but I'm gonna make you pay for the threat you were outside of these walls. I'm going to beat that pretty face of yours to a pulp. I'm going to inflict a punch for every one of us that you were responsible for putting away, and I'll reserve the hardest punch just for me."

Judd didn't flinch.

"You don't even remember me, do you?"

Judd made eye contact with Freeek for the first time. "Should I?"

"Yes, you fucking should. I'm a lifer because of you."

"You're a lifer because of you, you fucking dickhead. I'm doing my time because it was my fault, I get that. You're doing your time because it was your fault. Now live with it. You killed your missus. A defenceless woman who you terrified day in and day out. What did you expect a pat on the back?"

"So, you do remember me?"

"Yeah, I remember you. I always remember when I put a particular piece of scum behind bars. Domestic Violence, mate. Not a good image. I'd have thought you're nearly as unpopular in here as me. You're only one up from being a nonce."

Freeek gave out a large growl and pulled his fist back ready to strike. Once again Judd didn't flinch.

Suddenly a large thud came on the table, but this time it wasn't the hand of Freeek it was a prison officer's baton.

"Okay ladies, break this up. Freeek, turn around and walk away quietly."

Reluctantly, Freeek did as he was told, his lapdogs in tow.

Judd gave a sarcastic and childish wave. "Bye, Squeak."

This time it was the turn of the prison officer to lean into Judd. "Stone, pick your food up off the floor and don't make me ask twice."

CHAPTER 4
THE BARISTA

"What can I get you?" asked Sadie with her usual sweet delivery.

"Can I have a flat white coffee please and a slice of Red Velvet gateau."

"Sure thing, take a seat and I'll bring it over."

The boy smiled with both his mouth and his eyes. Sadie thought he was cute.

She watched him walk to the table by the window and sink his tall, slender frame into the chair. He faced the window so that he could look out towards the grounds of the university and Sadie watched him run his fingers through his mousey-coloured hair which was parted on the side. Eventually, she turned to prepare his drink.

The coffee shop hadn't been busy today. Sadie turned to her colleague. "Hey, Jolie. If we get a mad rush on can you hold the fort for a short while? I'm just gonna take this little lot to Hugh Grant's love child over there."

Jolie smiled. "Sure thing."

Sadie walked over towards the window seats. "Here you go, one flat white and a slice of Red Velvet gateau."

"Thank you, very much," he said looking alert and folding away his copy of the Financial Times.

"Wow, the Financial Times. You must be a real brain box," Sadie squirmed feeling a little embarrassed. *Is that the best you can do, girl?*

"Not really, I got kicked out of Oxford after all. That's why I find myself here at the University of Birmingham." Suddenly, the expression changed on his face to one of apprehension. "Oh, my goodness, how awful of me. I didn't even pay you, did I? What must you think of me?"

"I think you're pretty ok," Sadie couldn't believe how forward she was being. She turned red, she wasn't usually this confident but she was drawn to this boy like a chunk of metal to a magnet.

The boy smiled which melted Sadie even more. "That's very nice of you to say so. How much do I owe you?"

"Oh, forget it, it's on the house. Though with that accent you can't be short of a bob or two. Oh, sorry that came out wrong. What I meant was, you speak really nice."

The boy smiled again. "So, do you. I love the Birmingham accent."

"Really?"

"Really. It has such depth and character. The world would be a very boring place if everyone spoke like me. Please sit down and join me."

"Okay, just for a little while." Sadie looked back towards Jolie to check it was ok to leave her on her own for a while. The wink of an eye and a hand gesture of an 'OK' sign by her friend confirmed she approved.

"So, what's your name?" he asked.

"I'm Sadie, and yours?"

"Warwick."

"Blimey, even your name's posh. I'm very pleased to meet you, Warwick."

They shook hands for a short moment.

"The pleasure is all mine, Sadie."

"You once went to Oxford University you say? My

God, you must be so clever."

"Well, I couldn't get into Cambridge."

Sadie laughed.

"I prefer being here in Birmingham, to be honest."

"It's a friendly city. We Brummies are the salt of the earth as they say. I like working here at the uni too."

"Lucky for me that you do. Is this your coffee shop?"

"It's been a challenge competing with the big coffee chains, but yeah, it's mine."

"It's a great little place. How old are you, not that I should ever ask that of a lady?"

"I've never been called a lady before. I'm twenty-six."

"You're twenty-six and you run your own business. I'd say you're the clever one."

"I do ok, I guess. I would never have dreamed of ever going to a University such as Oxford though. You didn't tell me why you got kicked out."

"No, I didn't, did I."

CHAPTER 5
THE WARRIOR

"A six-month sentence and you're out in three. And they call that justice."

"I just kept my head down and done my time like any other prisoner."

"Yeah but you're not any other prisoner are you, Stone? You see I never much liked having a copper in my prison. I hated it almost as much as the inmates did."

"It was you who tried to break me, wasn't it? It was you who allowed mutants like Freeek to try and push my buttons. It would have made your day if my sentence had been increased wouldn't it?"

"You're a disgrace to your profession," spat the Governor.

"Ex-profession actually so I don't know why you're getting your Y-fronts in such a twist. Well, I'm sorry to disappoint you, Governor, you tried to break me but you failed. I'm out of here."

"Ok, Stone, you're right. You're free to go, all you have to do is walk out of that door ahead of you. But before you go there's someone who wants to say goodbye."

As the Governor spoke his words he turned to the door behind him, opened it and traded his exit for the entrance of a huge and familiar figure. Freeek moved slowly towards Judd grinning a manic grin through his overgrown beard. "Remember Stone, all you have to do is open that door and you're out of here. Good luck, you're going to need it."

"Hold on. If I fight this man it will get bloody. Are you telling me I can leave no matter what happens?"

"You have my word Stone. No matter how you achieve your aim, if you make it out of that door you're a free man. But you won't." The Governor closed the door behind him leaving the two men to face one another.

Freeek stood close to seven feet tall and seemed almost as wide. He had a smaller man stood either side of him in comparison, although they were still extremely well-built with black shiny bald heads and biceps that popped out like heads themselves.

"Me and my two pet baldies are gonna break you in half, Stone," growled Freeek. "The only way you're gonna be leaving this place is in a body bag."

Judd knew this was going to be the fight of his life and a mighty tough one. With a bear of a man like Freeek, there was only one surefire way to get the upper hand. Kick him as hard as he could in the balls! Judd's experience had taught him that it didn't matter how strong or weak a guy was, or how big or small, a sharp kick between the legs will hurt like hell for any given man. So that's exactly what he did and the huge frame of Freeek collapsed to his knees clutching at his agonising groin area.

Judd followed up on his assault on Freeek by throwing his rucksack which contained his few belongings at one of his assailants and then promptly and precisely catching the other one square on the lower jaw, knocking him unconscious and eliminating him from the rest of the fight.

The baldie who had been temporarily distracted due to Judd's flying rucksack charged at Judd and pinned him to the wall with a loud thud. Judd was winded and the baldie applied the pressure with a flurry of hard body punches. Judd managed to get a strong body punch in of his own which successfully diminished the attack on him but then he knew things were about to get much worse as he saw the massive frame of Freeek rise to its feet. And boy, did he look angry.

Judd hit the baldie again, this time in the face, but with one eye on Freeek, Judd let down enough guard for the slippery baldie to scramble behind him and grab him in a headlock.

The huge black bicep was having the desired effect as it pressed into Judd's Adam's apple and Judd began to feel himself losing consciousness. Through his blurry vision, he could make no mistake that the hulk of a man standing before him was Freeek and he felt the full force of the big man's fist strike his stomach.

"Hold that fucker still, Blizzard," and with those words, Freeek hit Judd a second time.

Struggling to breathe, Judd had to think fast if he was ever going to get out of this situation. Suddenly he remembered spotting something in Blizzard's right ear. With the huge arm around his neck, Judd was able to take advantage of the strong hold upon him and raised both his feet in order to kick Freeek in the stomach forcing the big man to fall flat on his rear. Then with lightning speed, Judd reached up behind his head and ripped the earring out of Blizzard's ear taking most of the earlobe with it. Judd followed up with a strong elbow to Blizzard's ribs and the noise of one of then breaking filled the air. Blizzard instinctively loosened his grip on Judd's neck and was soon sliding down the wall as Judd turned quickly to reverse the attack. Finally, Judd kicked him in the face three times in quick succession causing him to lose consciousness.

Judd turned around and Freeek had clumsily and slowly got to his feet.

"Right then you enormous piece of shit it's just you and me. Bring it on."

Incensed by Judd's provocation Freeek moved deliberately towards Judd. Judd, being the nimbler of the two, managed to strike the first blow by punching the big man in the chest hoping to break another rib or two but it had little effect. Hitting Freeek was like hitting a brick wall! Freeek retaliated and his powerful strike shook Judd but he just about managed to stay on his feet. However, his wobbly steps had taken him backwards and as Freeek moved towards him Judd searched his mind desperately on how he was going to survive this David and Goliath battle.

Relying on tried and tested methods Judd attempted to kick Freeek in the balls again but his opponent was wise this time and smacked the offending kick to one side with his huge shovel-like hand.

Judd decided that the best means of defence was to attack and he ran with speed and force at Freeek. Judd grabbed at Freeek's huge beard which forced the big man down to Judd's height allowing more of an even contest to unfold. Judd's advantage was his speed and he headbutted Freeek square on his already misshapen nose causing it to crack and bleed. This allowed enough time for Judd to run towards the door, knowing that if he could just get outside he would be free.

Judd reached the door unchallenged and placed one hand on the handle but as he did so Freeek with his giant steps had gained ground, grabbed Judd's shoulder and flung him across to the other side of the room. The huge man now stood squarely between Judd and the door to the outside world. Breathing heavily, Judd was desperate and didn't know quite what to do. It also crossed his mind that the two goons whom he had reduced to unconsciousness could wake up at any time and he doubted that his energy levels could cope with battling against three men again.

Judd took off his belt causing Freeek to laugh. "What are you going to do whip me to death you little prick?"

Using his advantage of speed once more Judd kicked Freeek hard in the knee causing the knee cap to pop out of its socket and the big man to collapse to a more manageable size. Judd moved swiftly behind Freeek and wrapped his belt around his throat pulling it as tight as he could. Freeek tried desperately to grab Judd, but Judd pinned his knee in the big man's back keeping it arched and ensuring he was always out of reach as he pulled tightly on the belt with all his might. Freeek's arms grasped in empty space like a dysfunctional windmill and eventually he lost his fight for life – and his fight with Judd Stone.

Victorious, Judd picked up his rucksack and left prison a free man.

CHAPTER 6
THE FORTUNE TELLER

It had proved difficult for a convicted ex-copper to find any meaningful work on the outside. Judd's skill-set had once allowed him to effectively combat crime using both his brawn and brains, but even though he had served his time, in the world of employment he felt as though he had remained in a virtual prison unable to shake loose his shackles of rejected opportunities. Judd's once exemplary police record now stood for nothing against his criminal one which meant all that remained in terms of a working day were the unsavoury areas of employment that could utilise the services he was able to provide.

Judd hated his job. But the reality was he simply needed some form of income in order to survive. For all his brashness and hot-headedness, deep down Judd Stone had always possessed a sweet soul and a kind heart. Being a debt-collector for a loan shark went somewhat against the grain.

As he knocked on the door of his latest 'customer', Judd took a moment of self-awareness and realised that he was even beginning to dress the part in his long dark woollen trench coat and heavy boots. *Good God, Stone, what happened to you?*

The door was originally designed to hold two glass panels each one separated by a single horizontal plank which should have harboured a letterbox but the letterbox was missing. The lower glass panel had been replaced by a piece of graffitied hardboard and Judd estimated that the last time the door and its frame had seen a lick of paint must have been at as long ago as the late seventies.

The door opened slowly and an eye surrounded by dark circles appeared in the opening. The gap was just wide enough for the predatory Judd Stone to force his foot in as a permanent wedge, much to the annoyance of the scrawny youth who had failed to close the door in time.

"What do you want?" said the youth.

"Two hundred quid, or at least my boss does."

"I don't have it?"

Judd rolled his eyes before fixing them menacingly on the young man. "That's just typical of the youth of today, isn't it? You want everything yesterday and you'll have it even if you can't afford it. Why don't muppets like you learn to live within their means and then you don't end up owing money to people like Ray Talia." Ray Talia was the younger brother of Gia Talia and was far less sophisticated than his big sister.

"I don't have the money."

Judd didn't bother answering, he simply forced the door open, stepped inside the property and closed the door behind him.

"Look I ain't got it. I can't give you what I ain't got can I, mister?"

Judd sighed. "So, what do you think is meant to happen now?"

"Look mate, beating me to a pulp ain't gonna get you the money is it?"

Judd grabbed the youth by the throat and forced him into the living room through the adjacent door.

"Well, let's see what we have here then. A large screen TV, a DVD player, a music system, a tropical fish tank. I could take any of these as part payment towards your debt. Tell me was it any of these things that possessed you to ask for the money in the first place? And if you tell me you needed the money for drugs I'm going to punch your lights out for being such a stupid boy."

"It was for my nana."

Judd loosened his grip. "Come again?"

"The money, it was for my nana?"

Suddenly a voice came from behind. "The boy speaks the truth; the money was for me."

Judd didn't quite know what to do. Money was owed to Ray Talia, a vicious and uncompromising individual and Judd clearly understood what his job specification entailed: get the cash off the punter in any way necessary and it's see you next time for the next over-inflated instalment; or if no payment is delivered, provide a lasting physical reminder to the customer regarding their debt and see you next time for your next over inflated instalment.

But there was no way on earth Judd was going to strike an old woman, or even strike her grandson in her presence. For all Judd's violent capabilities, unlike Ray, he did have a moral compass of sorts. Ray Talia, on the other hand, was simply a psychopath.

"What's your name, son? I don't exactly get paperwork with this loan outfit but I know of addresses, money owed and who originated the debt. I take it you're Justin?"

"I am."

"Ok Justin, stick the kettle on there's a good chap and let's see what we can work out here."

Judd took a sip of his tea. "Now you pair had better not be shitting me here. The loan is most definitely in your name Justin."

"I asked for the money for my Nana, I swear."

"He's a good boy, Mister…"

"You can call me, Judd. What did you need the money for, Nana?"

"And you can call me, Esmeralda."

"Is that really your name?"

"It is, and before you ask I don't know any hunchbacked bell-ringers."

Judd allowed himself to laugh.

"I have pancreatic cancer. Justin had heard about this new-fangled treatment in America with astounding results by all accounts. He is unemployed so he couldn't secure a loan in the usual way hence why he went to your boss. God knows I wish he hadn't. He collected the money as a surprise for me, he's a good boy, but if he had bothered to discuss it with me I'd have advised him never to bother. The irony is I flew to America on the borrowed money and after assessing my cancer they turned around and said they were very sorry but they couldn't do anything for me. The cancer was too aggressive."

"That's tough. How long do you have, Esmeralda?"

"Weeks, months, days. Who knows?"

"So, Justin borrowed all that money and the treatment in America was useless anyway?"

"For me personally, I'm afraid so," said Esmeralda.

Justin spoke next. "Luckily, I only borrowed the flight fare for us both, I wasn't gonna let Nana travel alone. The next step was to raise money to fund the treatment through sponsored events and social media pleas. The cost of the treatment would have run into tens of thousands of US dollars but the Americans informed us that in Nana's condition there was no point."

"I'm genuinely sorry to hear this," said Judd. "Your debt is written off, Justin."

"But I still owe almost two grand."

"Justin, when you take a loan out like yours you ultimately end up owing a lot more than you borrowed, but don't worry I'll make the debt go away."

"How?"

"I'll figure it out. Anyway, if you make me another cup of this fine tea that will more than meet the debt. Some things in life are priceless and a decent cuppa is one of them. You've found your vocation in life Justin, you make a great cup of tea. If you ever look to borrow cash again why not start up your own café business? But promise me that you will never, ever borrow money from the likes of Ray Talia again. There are people who can help with starting up businesses – the legitimate way."

"Thanks, Judd," said Justin. "Are you being serious, I really don't owe any more money?"

"Correct. You did a wonderful thing for your nana, next time just think through your good intentions a bit more, eh?"

"I will."

Esmeralda took Judd's hand.

"When you were threatening the boy, I came very close to putting a curse on you Judd, but the instant I looked into your eyes I saw kindness."

"A curse?"

"I'm from a family of gypsies, Judd. I'm related to the gypsy that placed a curse on the Birmingham City football stadium which could only be lifted by peeing in all four corners of St Andrews."

"Really?" Judd was aware of the gypsy curse that had been associated with the Blues' lack of good fortune in the world of football.

"In fact, I was the first of my family to give up the travelling lifestyle and settle down in a house. Well, actually it was Justin's parents that orchestrated it all. My daughter and her husband. They moved into this house and had me move in with them about twenty-five years ago"

"Where are they now?"

"Killed in a boating accident I'm afraid. It means I brought up young Justin here from a very early age."

"That's why I'd do anything for my nana."

Still holding Judd's hand Esmeralda continued. "I'd

read your tea leaves, Judd but I can't get anything from tea bags so I'll read your palm instead. You'll be glad to know you have a very healthy lifeline, you've years ahead of you yet Judd."

"Yes, I'm pleased to learn that."

"Nana, Judd deserves the full treatment, don't you think?"

"You're right, Justin."

Judd frowned not exactly sure what 'the full treatment' entailed. Esmeralda released Judd's hand and got up from the ageing sofa. She walked slowly across the small living room and bent down to the lower left-hand cupboard of the sideboard. Teak in colour Judd estimated that the sideboard was a product of the 1980's. Well-made but outdated in a big way. Esmerelda rolled out a velvet looking cloth on the dining table and placed upon it a globe of glass."

"You're kidding me? A crystal ball?"

"Come and sit over here, Judd. Let's see what the future has in store for you."

Judd complied, and as he sat down he wasn't really sure if he wanted to know what was in store for him. He concluded he'd just go through the motions to please Esmeralda and Justin, but would take what was said with a pinch of salt. He wasn't convinced that fortune tellers really existed, not via the use of a crystal ball anyway. Surely this was just fairground attraction stuff, no-one ever really took this kind of thing seriously. Did they?

Esmeralda danced her hands over the thick glass ball, "I see that sweet soul of yours Judd, hidden deep within you, but you have hurt someone very close to you."

Judd knew who Esmeralda was referring to. Brooke. But then again what Esmerelda was saying could be attributed to the majority of society, it was hardly a staggering revelation and perhaps just an educated guess by those who claim to be able to read lives.

Esmeralda continued seemingly getting lost in the

crystal ball before her as if it was becoming an extension of her own being. "I see a girl and I hear music, but this girl is much younger than the one you've hurt. She is very different and creative compared to the average person and she is very special. She is in danger, Judd and only you can help her."

Judd concluded that Esmeralda's words were nothing more than claptrap. Judd figured that Esmerelda believed what she was saying and wasn't necessarily being dishonest but he just didn't buy it. How could he help a girl in danger? After all, he was no longer a copper.

Esmeralda's stare into the glass dome gained an even stronger focus. "The music is getting stronger and I see a number. The number is 9. I don't quite know the implication of the number 9 but it is significant, Judd. Someone is in danger and music and the number 9 play a huge part in the situation that is about to come your way."

"Are you sure it's a girl in danger, not a bloke?"

Esmerelda concentrated hard on the glass ball. Judd couldn't help but notice the intensity in her stare as her fingers continued to hover and flutter above the sphere.

"I sense that the person in danger is most definitely of a female origin. And the number 9 is at the centre of this girl's peril."

Suddenly Esmerelda broke her stare and fell back into the chair appearing exhausted.

"I'm sorry Judd, due to my ill health my fortune telling is not as precise as it once was."

"It's ok, Esmerelda."

"You don't believe what I saw do you, Judd?"

Judd wanted to remain polite. "It's not that I don't believe Esmeralda, I just don't understand yet, but that's the essence of fortune telling, isn't it? I can't see into the future that's all so it's hard for me to recognise what you are telling me. It's not that I doubt you or your intentions. The reading was very interesting. Tell me, do you ever detect anything from the past?"

"Sometimes."

"Mmmm, that would make more sense perhaps in what you've seen. Anyway, it was lovely to meet you both, unfortunately, I've spent far too much time here and I must move on to my next customer."

"Victim you mean?" shot Esmerelda. "You don't need to do this job, Judd. You are a better man than this."

"Beggars can't be choosers, Esmerelda. I need to pay bills too you know."

"There are other ways, and your gift is to help people, even if it is in the most unconventional way at times."

Judd stood up from his seat, leaned over to Esmerelda and kissed her on the cheek. "You take care, now."

He walked towards the entrance of the house. "Justin, do us all a favour and think before you get yourself into a mess like this again."

"I will, Judd. Are you sure the debt is over."

"It's over. Leave it with me. I'll see myself out."

Once Judd was outside he pulled up the collars of his long coat as the chill of the air instantly hit him.

He stood on the path for a while digesting Esmerelda's words. If it hadn't been mumbo-jumbo that she had been spouting, he was convinced that the most likely explanation was that it had been the past that she had focused on. The need to help a girl? Take your pick he thought. From his deceased wife Frankie who had been murdered by Delroy Whitton, an ex-con who Judd had ensured had been put away to make the streets of Birmingham a lot safer at the time. Judd had failed to reach Frankie in time to save her but Whitton had been tortured and made to pay for his ill-fated choice to kill the wife of Judd Stone. And before Frankie, there had been Bonnie, another girl he was all too acutely aware that he had failed to protect. Bonnie had been raped at the hands of Marlon Howell, the disgraced England Football manager and ex-footballing hero whom Judd had once again retrospectively ensured that justice had prevailed.

The guilt still ate away at Judd for both Frankie and Bonnie. Yes, revenge had been sweet but the failure to prevent the acts is what killed him inside.

Judd had also helped bring justice to the victims of serial killer Gareth Banks, aka *The Crucifier*. Is this what Esmerelda had hit upon in her confused state of mind when she said he had to protect a girl? Living with terminal pancreatic cancer can't be easy and it must have an all-encompassing effect on one's health? Judd could only imagine the pain Esmerelda must be going through on a daily basis both physically and mentally.

But Judd questioned that if she can see into the future why doesn't she know exactly when her time is up? She had referred to her own death to be days, weeks or months. Her exact prognosis was unknown. But then again, he had often asked much the same of Crystal, his good friend William's partner who was a medium. In this, he didn't doubt. Why don't you predict the lottery numbers, Crystal? Judd would playfully ask her. Her answer being "It doesn't quite work like that, you rascal."

And what about the music connection and the number 9 that Esmerelda had spoken of? What was that all about?

Then it hit Judd like the opening bars of Prince's "When Doves Cry".

Screw me sideways, perhaps the woman does have something?

Judd remembered that a certain man had been born on the 9th day of October, as was this man's second son.

The same man's first home had been number 9 Newcastle Road.

And he met the influential manager of the band that he founded and his second wife five years apart on the 9th day of November.

That same band made its first appearance at The Cavern Club on 9 February 1961.

When it was time to take America by storm the band appeared on the Ed Sullivan Show exactly three years later on 9 February 1964.

He wrote at least three well-known songs which featured the number 9 in their song title, including #9 Dream, following a dream that he had experienced.

After being shot on 8 December 1980 he had been rushed to Roosevelt Hospital on 9th Avenue, Manhattan.

He died on that 8 December 1980 due to the fatal gunshot wounds robbing the world of an immense talent and voice that went far beyond music – which due to the time difference meant that he died on 9 December in his native Liverpool, England.

The footballer from his childhood drawing which appeared on the cover of the *Walls and Bridges* album had a number 9 on the back of his shirt. When Judd Stone was an up and coming footballer he too often wore the number 9 shirt.

For Judd it now made sense. Esmerelda had tapped into Judd's psyche and had unearthed his deep admiration for John Lennon, the musician who had been obsessed and almost defined by the number 9.

CHAPTER 7
THE NEW FRIEND

Judd slammed down the bulky brown envelope onto the desk.

"What's this?" asked Ray Talia.

"Two grand exactly, the remainder of Justin Corrigan's debt. He's fully paid up."

"I'll say when he's fully paid up, there may be some interest owing."

"He's fully paid up. How often do you get a debt paid back in full? The kid was only trying to help his sick old grandma, cut him some slack."

"When that kid took that money from me…"

"Borrowed, not took."

"Whatever. He didn't seem to have the means to cover the instalments. He was my kind of punter. The vulnerable dickhead kind."

"You've got your money now, Ray. What does it matter?"

"I'm just curious, that's all. How does a pikey like that suddenly got the means to pay an instalment let alone clear the debt? You're not going soft in your old age are you

Judd?"

"Don't be daft. How should I know how he got the money? I didn't ask."

"Perhaps your reputation about breaking fingers, noses and legs reached him when people don't pay me what they owe, Judd. Perhaps hearing about that was enough for him to cough up."

"Maybe. Maybe not. In any case, I don't want this job no more."

Ray looked perplexed. "Really? Even though you're so good at it? You're very effective Judd at getting results."

"It's not ethical."

"Fuck me, Judd Stone is developing a conscience all of sudden? Listen Judd, I decide when your services are no longer required, and you ain't going nowhere without my say so. People don't just work for me, I fucking own them."

"Well you're gonna have to disown me, Ray."

"Look here, Stone. Your days of calling any shots finished the day they booted you off the force. You work for me now and it's not as if I don't pay you well, but that's because you do a good job. I've plenty more customers who need the powers of your persuasion."

"I plan to leave on a high, Ray. I've got you two grand there. You've got plenty more meatheads on the payroll to do your dirty work for you."

Ray stroked his chin giving the impression he was a thinking man but in reality, he lacked a great deal of intelligence. He ruled by fear and he owed any success he had to that. To that and his sister's far more superior credibility, wiliness and recognised respect in the world of gangsters. She had even managed to evade all the charges that had been stacking up against her in spite of the intense undercover operation that had been deployed by Birmingham and District CID. Police officers and witnesses had been paid off. Families had been threatened by the Talia regime. And others who had got in the way had suffered a much worse fate.

"Ok, Judd. To be honest, I've never been fully comfortable having ex-filth work for me. In fact, I took quite a lot of stick hiring you. I simply did my sister a favour, she likes you for some fucked-up reason and I reckon she wanted me to keep tabs on you just in case she was to end up behind bars, though she'd never admit to it of course. In truth, I've started to warm to your charms too. But you're still old bill at the end of the day which causes certain disharmony in my workforce."

"Well if I walk away now we both get what we want, don't we?"

Suddenly Judd heard a movement in the corner of the room. This was followed by a long sigh as the animal got comfortable. Judd had failed to notice that a third party had been present until now.

"Who's your friend?" asked Judd.

"That is no friend of mine, the useless little shit. He's cost me money. Lots of it. He's lucky he's still alive. I don't quite know what to do with him."

"Well, I can see that the dog is no greyhound and judging by those battle scars you've been using him for dogfighting, haven't you?"

"Yeah, but his time is done before it's even got properly started. He had one fight and lost. I'll probably get one of the boys to drown the little fuck. I thought he may die of his injuries but he's a resilient little fucker I'll give him that. Unlike the other dogs we've had, this mutt seems to have a conscience. Makes him a bit like you hey Stone? He can fight alright but he has a gentle side to him which cost him the fight in the end. He couldn't finish the kill when he had it in his sights. He let the other fucker off the hook. He lacks the old eye of the tiger. I can't be arsed with him. If he hasn't got that natural aggression he's never gonna make me any serious dough."

"I'll get rid of him for you if we agree to part company. Call it one last favour. Does he have a name?"

"Apart from useless little prick. Nah. We don't give them names Judd. They're not fucking pets."

Judd walked over to the dog in the corner. The dog growled initially, the experience in his short life so far resulting in any human presence being taken to be an enemy. Then the dog began to sense an air of decency from the big man who kneeled down beside him.

"There's a good boy," said Judd as he placed the back of his hand in front of the dog's face, allowing him to sniff it. Soon after Judd was stroking the dog's head.

"What are you fussing it for? I thought you were gonna kill the useless piece of shit for me."

"It'll be far easier to do the job if the dog thinks he can trust me, Ray. If he's being a lot less resistant towards me then I can do the deed when he's least expecting it."

"Whatever, just get the useless fuck out of my sight."

"Do you have a lead?" asked Judd as he stood to his feet.

"No, just the chain he's got around his scrawny little neck."

Judd messed with the chain and managed to free one end from the old Victorian radiator and began to walk with the dog, who followed as good as gold even though he clearly had a limp from his battle.

"I guess this is goodbye then, Judd. Don't expect any forwarding wages. I'll see you around."

I hope not thought Judd. "Yeah see you around, Ray."

Once outside Judd fussed the dog some more. "Don't worry fella, I ain't gonna harm you. I just needed to trick that nasty prick back there so I could get you out of that place, luckily, he's so fucking dumb he's easy to fool. I can give you a home, I'm gonna take care of you in the proper sense of the phrase." Judd gently searched the dog's fur and became concerned with the wounds that were present on the poor animal. "I'll get these cuts sorted too. I'll get you registered with a proper vet. Luckily, I can see they're healable, you're gonna be ok. You're a tough little lad ain't ya? A tough dog with a gentle side. Mmmm, yeah, you remind me of me alright. I'll get you a nice collar too, I'll get rid of this nasty old chain as soon as I can. I tell you what, I feel like wrapping it around that lowlife Ray Talia's neck. That psycho really is a piece of work. Come on boy, let's go home."

As Judd and his new companion entered further into the daylight, Judd could see that the dog possessed some attractive colourings and markings amongst his cuts. The dog had Staffordshire Bull Terrier in him for sure, a dog breed that originated in Birmingham – another similarity to Judd, but curiously there seemed to be an ancestry link to the Border Collie breed somewhere along the line, giving the dog a longer length of fur than a standard pedigree "Staffie". There was an attractive mixture of three colours in the dog's coat: black, white and the predominant colour of rusty reddish-brown. The mixture of dog breeds was most likely the reason why he lacked the killer instinct to be an underground fighting dog.

During his time as a detective, Judd had found great pleasure in bringing those responsible for dog fighting to justice – in his own imitable style, of course, most of the time. He could never understand why anyone would want to hurt either an animal or a child. Needless to say, abusers of children also got their just desserts when Judd had been on the case. In Judd's mind, animals and children were of an innocent standing and as such, any crime that had been committed against them deserved the perpetrator to be punished to the maximum level possible where Judd was concerned.

"So, what am I gonna call you, kid? I'm a bit of a Beatle's fan, but Paul, George or John ain't a great name for a dog is it? How about Ringo? That could work, yeah?"

The dog whimpered slightly. "Oh, ok so you don't like the name, Ringo. If you were a girl dog I could call you Pam after the song 'Polythene Pam'. It's a song on one of my favourite albums, *Abbey Road*. You'll hear it over and over coming to live with me."

Judd had a quick scan of the environment around him. Both he and the dog were still alone.

"Listen to me talking to a dog, can you understand anything I say?"

The dog cocked his head attentively to one side.

"Hey I've got it, how about Mr. Mustard? There's another song on that very same album called 'Mean Mr. Mustard'. Not that you're mean or anything."

The dog barked approvingly.

"Well there ya go then. Mr. Mustard it is. Come on Mr. Mustard let's go home."

Following the loss of Brooke, Judd had no proper girl to call his own, and he didn't feel that he could count the very casual intermittent relationship that he had with a certain notorious female gangster. He had no job and was now two grand lighter in his savings account - nothing he couldn't rectify by indulging in a game or two of cards he figured.

But at least he now had a new friend.

CHAPTER 8
THE MAN WITH THE UMBRELLA

These days Judd had moved from his home in the centre of Sutton Coldfield to a plush apartment on the twentieth floor of the Rotunda building. The Rotunda, an iconic cylindrical construction much loved by Brummies new and old, has dominated the Birmingham city skyline since 1965. Securing the apartment when he was Detective Chief Inspector Stone, the payments were proving difficult now he was bringing in much more elusive earnings. Fortunately, for all the bad luck Judd had been experiencing, he did at least currently find himself on a bit of a winning streak concerning his gambling activity. It was a good job he was winning more than he was losing because living in the Grade II Listed Rotunda was not a cheap option. But how long that situation would last was anyone's guess?

Judd looked out of his high-rise window. He was never disappointed with the panoramic views of Birmingham that were on offer. Since his move to the Rotunda, he often wasted a considerable number of minutes taking in his immediate surroundings and beyond. The positioning of Judd's apartment meant he could watch the trains pull into Birmingham New Street Station as well as embracing a bird's eye view of one of the futuristic-looking pedestrian entrances of the stylish Grand Central shopping complex which has enveloped the station since 2015.

Or if he preferred he could witness the swarms of people pass along New Street itself or towards a portion of the Bull Ring. Judd's view also enabled him to have sight of the rear walls and yard of the Odeon cinema. This rear location of the Odeon cinema had once been frequented by the best musicians of the day. The Odeon is nostalgically recognised as being one of the most significant and thriving music venues in Birmingham's musical history and has hosted some major musical heavyweights such as Abba, Bob Marley, Elvis Costello, Human League, Led Zeppelin, Status Quo and U2 to name just a few.

Judd's eyes caught sight of a bright pink Hummer and he followed its ascendance turning into Hurst Street, the gateway to Birmingham's China Town, Gay Village and the Arcadian night scene which were all intertwined in that particular location of the city. Judd guessed that the inhabitants sat behind the blacked-out windows of the vehicle were most likely the gathering of a Hen party that was starting incredibly early with their celebrations, or perhaps it was an assembly of folk about to attend the nearby Birmingham Hippodrome to take in an evening's entertainment of the latest hit musical which was on show. Suddenly his concentration was broken as the buzzing sound of his intercom kicked in indicating that someone was at the entrance of the tubular building.

"Hello," he said placing the receiver to his ear.

Judd was surprised to hear the voice at the other end of the line. He recognised it immediately.

"You'd better come up. Take the lift or you'll be a while."

Three minutes or so later DSI Ben Francis was

standing in the living room of Judd Stone's Rotunda apartment.

"You're looking well, Judd. Considering…"

"Considering I was kicked off your precious force, you mean? Yeah, thanks for nothing."

"That's not fair, Judd. You know I tried to save your skin but you had made the situation impossible."

Judd shrugged. "So, what brings you here, and who's this?"

"This is my niece on my wife's side. Say hello, Xanthe."

"Hello," said the girl not making eye contact. Judd estimated her age to be less than twenty years old, but definitely someone who had left her school years behind.

"Hi, Xanthe. You have a nice name."

The girl didn't respond.

Ben continued.

"I think you can help us, Judd. Or help Xanthe in any case."

"Me, help you? How's that then?"

"Xanthe has certain, how shall I say, obsessions. She's highly intelligent, Judd and she believes she's onto something but I'm not so sure."

"Onto something? Are you a copper too, Xanthe?" asked Judd.

Xanthe still avoided eye contact but this time she answered. "That's a strange thing to ask. I am neither a metal which is reddish-orange in colour or a chemical element with the symbol Cu taken from the Latin cuprum."

Judd frowned. The girl seemed deadly serious in her speech, almost formal, and she genuinely appeared to interpret Judd's question in connection with copper metal and not the slang word for a policeman.

Judd noticed Ben smiling. "Xanthe takes things very literally, Judd." Ben then turned to Xanthe. "Judd was just wondering if you were a police officer like your uncle here."

CLUB 27

This time it was Xanthe's turn to frown.

"My uncle says you can help me, Mr. Stone. He claims that you and your friend Mr. Chamberlain were the best detectives that he ever knew, however, Mr. Chamberlain is suffering from ill health at the moment and shouldn't be disturbed."

"Well, that's very kind of you to say Xanthe, but your uncle is a serving detective. Why can't he help you?"

"He doesn't believe what I am telling him, even though I have clearly presented the facts."

"Believe you? About what?"

"The 27 club. Someone is in grave danger and my uncle told me that if anyone can help them then you can. You prevented a celebrity from being killed before. Your experience and unconventional application of methods are second to none in helping the person in danger and ensuring that the 27 club doesn't claim another victim."

Judd noticed how Xanthe spoke elegantly but with a very rhythmic delivery. She still hadn't made eye contact with him.

"The 27 club?" Judd looked puzzled.

"The 27 club is the term given to the unusual amount of musicians that have died at the tender age of 27. The first recognised member of the club is usually attributed to Alexandre Levy, a Brazilian composer and pianist who died on 17 January 1892. The cause of his death is unknown. Of course, many musicians have died prematurely but the increased amount at the age of 27 is remarkable and beyond coincidence. Brian Jones of the Rolling Stones, Alan 'Blind Owl' Wilson, Jimi Hendrix, Janis Joplin and Jim Morrison all died within an exact window of three years. Both Jones and Morrison were claimed on the third day of July, 1969 and 1971 respectively. But it didn't stop there, you will be familiar Mr. Stone of the more recent deaths of Kurt Cobain and Amy Winehouse."

"Now that you come to mention it Xanthe, I have

heard of the 27 club as it happens. However, my knowledge on the subject is far more inferior than your own. I'm quite a fan of Amy Winehouse as it goes."

"It doesn't stop with Amy and it won't ever stop. More recently members of the indie bands Viola Beach and Surfer Blood died at the age of 27.

"Phoenix Easter is arguably the most renowned singer-songwriter of her generation. Her unique talent and reckless approach to life make her a classic candidate to be the next member."

"You don't know that for sure, Xanthe," interjected Ben.

"Oh, yes I do. All the evidence is considerably stacking up to place Phoenix as the next member."

"Phoenix Easter. Really? She rocks. A local heroine too. How old is she?" asked Judd.

"Twenty-six years of age."

"I see why you're concerned. But your Uncle is correct, Xanthe. She could go on performing into her seventies yet. Eighties even."

"Uncle Ben, will you show Mr. Stone the photographs please?"

"Photos?"

Ben pulled a tablet from his jacket pocket which was deep enough to hold the device. "This is where my niece can be very persuasive Judd, and believe me, you are going to find what I'm about to show you quite staggering."

"Let's sit down," offered Judd. "Sorry I should have offered earlier."

Ben and Judd sat closely together on the sofa so that they could comfortably share the view of the tablet screen, whilst Xanthe chose not to sit. Instead, she walked behind the sofa and stood over the two men oblivious to invading any personal space. To Xanthe, it made perfect sense to manoeuvre to a position where she too could see the pictures that were about to unfold across the screen.

"You'll have no difficulty in recognising the first

picture, Judd," said Ben.

It was a photo that Judd had seen many times and his anger on seeing it never seemed to diminish. It was the chilling picture that captured John Lennon signing a copy of his album *Double Fantasy* for the man who just hours later would kill him in almost the same spot.

"The audacity of that bastard still makes me sick while Lennon unsuspectingly signs his album. Lennon was aged forty when he was killed though, where's the 27 connection?"

"There isn't one, Judd," said Ben. "The significance of this photo is the sinister presence of the third party in the photo. He's very hard to spot in this particular picture and many never spot him at all he's so inconspicuous. He's very far away in the distance and the average sizing when this photo is displayed loses him altogether in the diminished pixels, but he's there. But just hold that thought as a concept as we look at the other pictures that I have."

Ben swiped the images from right to left and next a very grainy picture appeared. Judd could make out that to the right of the picture was a motorcade complete with a number of people in and around the vehicle. A less amount of people were standing to the left of the picture.

"This photo is from one of the most significant days in history, Judd, but do you notice anything unusual?"

"My guess is it's the day of the JFK shooting."

"Yes, it is. This picture was taken just moments before the president was shot. But I'll ask you again, my friend. Do you spot anything unusual?"

"Not really."

"Are you sure? You haven't lost your detective skills already have you? Remember this was a very sunny day in Texas."

Judd concentrated on the picture for a couple more seconds and then he did notice something amiss. "Well fuck me sideways. Why has that guy got an umbrella up?"

"Exactly."

"I'm not sure how old JFK was when he was killed but I'm sure he was older than 27."

"All will become clear Judd. Now let me show you some photos of the recognised members of the 27 club."

Judd watched with interest as Ben swiped images in and out of the screen, each photo displaying a famous person who had met their untimely death at the age of 27. They included a picture each of Jim Morrison, Jimi Hendrix, Kurt Cobain, Brian Jones, Amy Winehouse, Janis Joplin, the rappers known as Stretch and Fredo Santana and a few more.

"Wow, all of those talented people died at the tender age of 27. It is unbelievable when you stop and think about it," said Judd.

"It certainly is," said Ben. "Tragic too. But did you notice anything similar with each of the photos, Judd?"

"Well none of them were professional photos taken at any studio photo shoot. They had all been taken in public places, quite randomly it would seem."

"That's correct which meant that our famous person was not the only person in the pictures although they were the main focus of course. Now, I'm going to show you the same photos again Judd, but this time ignore the famous face within and concentrate on the other elements of the photo."

"Ok."

"So, close your mind to the obvious feature of the photo and it will become clear."

Judd closed his eyes and then opened them again to begin afresh.

Judd concentrated on the photos for a second time. This time as they moved back and forth before him his jaw physically dropped with the realisation of their common denominator.

"My God. The guy with the umbrella. He's in the background of every single one of these photos."

"Indeed, Judd. Quite remarkable really."

"Remarkable and chilling."

"Agreed. Well, it's either the same person or simply another person who is dressed the same as our man in Dallas in 1963. I mean, can it really be the very same man holding aloft an umbrella in Camden Town in 2011 just a few days before Amy Winehouse passed away? I'm not ruling out it is the same man even with the passage of time, because if there is something supernatural about all of these deaths at the age of 27 then I guess anything is possible. Xanthe certainly believes so."

"Whether it is the same dude or not, the significant thing is, is that all of these stars who died at the age of 27 had a photograph unwittingly taken with a mysterious umbrella holder accompanying them. Chillingly the photos seem to suggest that the presence of the Umbrella Man acts like some sort of prophecy of their deaths."

"That's about it, Judd."

"It sends shivers down your spine."

"Even Alexandre Levy who died all those years ago had a note in his journal that refers to the presence of a mysterious man with a black umbrella in the days leading up to his death. Why would you need an umbrella in Brazil?"

"It's pretty mind-blowing. But this guy carrying a black umbrella has featured in pictures of people who did not die at the age of 27. Like I've said already, JFK wasn't 27."

Xanthe decided to speak. "John Fitzgerald Kennedy the 35th president of the United States was assassinated at 12.30pm Central Standard Time on Friday 22 November 1963. The fifth day of the week plus the twenty-second day of the month equals 27. Or to look at it another way, the killing took place at 12.30pm in the eleventh month of 1963. 1+2+3+0+1+1+1+9+6+3 equals 27. The number 27 dominates the assassination. He wasn't a musician or an artist, but his presidency was more showbiz and transcended social culture more than any other up until that point. For example, he famously kept the company of Hollywood legends Marilyn Monroe and Frank Sinatra."

"Xanthe believes that the 27 club reaches beyond just the age of the person. It's all about the number 27 itself too as the vital ingredient. To my knowledge, I don't believe anyone other than Xanthe has ever made this connection."

"Show Mr. Stone the other photos, Uncle Ben."

Judd was shown pictures of Marvin Gaye, Peter Tosh, Chester Bennington and George Michael. All four photos had the Umbrella Man lurking in the background.

"Unbelievable. But again, these guys weren't 27 when they died, so where's the connection with the number?"

Xanthe once again revealed all. "Motown legend Marvin Gaye was shot dead by his father on April 1 1984. 4+1+1+9+8+4 equals 27. Reggae star Peter Tosh was killed September 11 1987. 1+1+1+9+8+7 equals 27. George Michael broke hearts all over the world when he passed away on Christmas Day 2016 at the untimely age of 53. 5+3+2+5+1+2+2+0+1+6 equals 27."

Judd was able to tap into the unfolding theme. "And Chester Bennington took his own life on 20 July. The twentieth day of the seventh month equaling 27."

"Now you're following, Judd," said Ben. "My niece has the ability to focus on certain subjects very intensely, the 27 club being one of them. She's pretty convincing wouldn't you say?"

"I certainly would. Her commitment to detail and subject matter knowledge is incredible."

"There is another Club 27 connection with George Michael," said Xanthe.

"Go on," encouraged Judd.

"Pete DeFreitas was a drummer with Echo and the Bunnymen and he was killed in a road traffic accident on the A51 in Staffordshire at the age of 27."

"So, he is another recognised member of the 27 club, but I don't quite follow, Xanthe. Where is the George

Michael connection?"

"The ashes of Pete DeFreitas are buried in the village of Goring-On-Thames. Goring-On-Thames was where George Michael was discovered dead in his riverside home."

"Wow, that is a chilling coincidence."

"Pete DeFreitas was in one of those photographs that I showed you," said Ben. "Not every star who dies is a member of the 27 club. But every member of the 27 club has the Umbrella Man appear in their photos moments, days or weeks before their untimely deaths. Why the famous people are chosen remains a mystery. Why the number 27 is significant remains a mystery. The presence of the Umbrella Man remains a mystery. But although they are mysteries, either yet to be solved or perhaps never to be solved they remain facts. I have one more photo to show you."

Ben revealed a picture of a beautiful girl born from mixed-parentage who had been typically caught in a vulnerable state by the paparazzi. The state of her pupils suggested that she had taken drugs and she was sticking her middle finger to the photographer in question. Behind her stood a man whose features could not be distinguished but he was clearly holding aloft an open umbrella. The photo had been taken at night time, and although it was dark, twenty-six-year-old Phoenix Easter's bleached hair being in a state of dryness suggested that it hadn't been raining.

"I can't justify deploying resource to follow any of this up, Judd. Where would I begin to convince the force to take all of this seriously? I'd be laughed out of the station."

"I see your point, Ben. But if Phoenix were to die at the age of 27 how bad would you feel, after listening to Xanthe?"

"Pretty bad."

"That's why I need you to help me Mr. Stone." Xanthe kept her head down as she spoke but her statement seemed genuine.

"Xanthe, how can I help? I'm unemployed at the moment. I have no regular income, and in fact, I'd prefer your uncle wasn't here if I were to explain how I'm currently making ends meet."

"But you have enough money to feed your dog," said Xanthe bluntly. The girl had still not made any eye contact with Judd in all this time.

"Well yeah. Man's best friend and all that. Mr. Mustard's predicament was even worse than mine when we met."

"You helped Mr. Mustard, your dog. I can tell you are a kind man. That's why I know you can help Phoenix Easter."

"But how?"

Ben Francis spoke. "Judd, you were a fantastic copper. A little rough around the edges, a little unconventional but believe me the streets of Birmingham were a lot safer when you were on the Force. I've always felt responsible for you in many ways. I liked you and I liked having you around. I'm sorry I couldn't save your ass that one final time."

"Water under the bridge, Ben. I'm sorry I had a pop at you earlier. I made my own bed not you."

"Nevertheless, as I've stated I can't use B.A.D CID on this project but I could use you, if you're willing. I will fund your investigation to protect Phoenix Easter from becoming the next member of the 27 Club."

"Well, I could sure do with the money, and a job for that matter. Ben Francis going bent. I thought I'd never see the day."

"Not bent Judd, merely funding an unorthodox investigation utilising the best man I can think of for this particularly unusual project. You've saved the ass of a celebrity before remember."

"Yeah, Marlon Howell. I'd rather have seen him hang if possible."

"You brought him to justice while saving his life. It was a good result all round and one that should have been better remembered at the time of your dismissal. So what d'ya say?"

Judd looked at Xanthe who still had her head hanging down. If he could have looked into her eyes for just a second Judd knew that he would have seen a state of desperation in them. And cruelly disappointing a young girl so full of hope was never his style. The look in her eyes would have been more than enough to convince him to take this job. And anyway, what did he have to lose?

By now it had also occurred to Judd that Esmeralda had seemed to earn a sense of credibility in all of this. She had spoken to Judd about the number 9 which he had taken to mean something connected with his hero John Lennon who had been dominated by that number throughout his life.

It now occurred to Judd following Xanthe's expert analysis of the number 27 that the significance of a number can also include the numerical ingredients of it.

If we were to take the number nine for example. Lennon would catch the number 72 bus with his best mate Stu Sutcliffe in order to get to art college. The Dakota where Lennon lived and was sadly killed outside was on New York's West 72nd Street and his apartment in the Dakota had been number 72.

Adding the numbers 7 and 2 together had made the number 9, thus it was still a constant in Lennon's life through the essence of basic arithmetic.

Esmerelda had stated he needed to help a girl in danger. Music was heavily connected in the situation as was the number nine.

The girl could easily be Phoenix Easter. Phoenix is a musician of the highest order. Her next birthday would make her 27 years of age, the distinct age that tragically many well-known musicians curiously meet their untimely death. 2 plus 7 equals 9.

Judd looked at his friend and smiled. "I say yes."

CHAPTER 9
THE HUNTER

During a separate encounter on the telephone, Ben Francis had explained to Judd the reasoning for Xanthe's intense focus concerning the 27 Club. His niece had Asperger's Syndrome, a form of autism which enables her to possess an above average intellect and an incredible ability to obsess about a subject that may seem unusual to those outside of her thinking. Xanthe's fascination focused on the 27 Club.

Unfortunately, Xanthe's condition also had its challenges. Her Asperger's Syndrome often made it tough to fit in with her peer groups. Jokes and punchlines would obliviously pass over her head and she repeatedly found it difficult to understand the intent behind sarcasm or irony. Instead, Xanthe would always take things very literally just as she had done when Judd had referred to a 'copper' being a policeman. To Xanthe, a policeman could be the only possible term for a policeman and copper had to be a reddish-brown metal and nothing else. Xanthe was also unable to recognise the unwritten rules naturally established around social interaction. She could be unwittingly blunt and unaware of hurting people's feelings yet she could be agonisingly shy. Judd realised now why Ben's niece had found it so challenging to make eye contact.

But Xanthe was also naturally astute and her notions around the 27 club needed to be taken seriously. Ben Francis knew this. But while Ben realised he would be unable to convince the Force to seriously get involved, coupled with the lack of resource available to apply to such an outlandish investigation when the daily crimes of Birmingham were not going to go away any time soon, he realised that the evidence presented by Xanthe was credible enough to follow through - hence the reaching out to the most ground-breaking detective he had ever known: Judd Stone. It was quite a simple match really once Ben had worked it out – an unconventional investigation required an unconventional investigator.

Meanwhile, Warwick and Sadie had enjoyed getting to know one another a little better since their meeting at Sadie's coffee shop located on the University of Birmingham campus. The odd trip into town for shopping at the Bull Ring and Grand Central shopping centres, or drinks at the many bars and pubs on offer, had set an amicable enough foundation for the next natural progression of their relationship.

Sadie couldn't believe that Warwick had asked her to stay at his actual home for the weekend. Home was a sixteen-roomed mansion near Stow-on-the-Wold, Gloucestershire, set within its own acres of splendid greenery. A gravel driveway sat behind the iron gates of the mansion and Sadie had noticed the Jaguar cars and other expensive cars and 4x4 vehicles come and go from the window of the room she had been allocated. Sadie considered the room to be gorgeous with its William Morris patterns dominating the expensive décor and bright-white dressing table – which just happened to be the largest and grandest dressing table that she had ever seen. And the room was only one of several potential guest rooms in this impressive house.

Some of the cars she had spotted belonged to Warwick's family members: Mom, Dad, siblings and even cousins but Warwick's parents were clearly big noises in this vicinity if the vast amount of visitors was anything to go by.

On this particular morning, Sadie looked out of the window to witness Warwick's father step from his house to join a gathering of folk who were patiently waiting in the forecourt. The gathering were sporting a variety of jackets either treated with wax or made from tweed and their feet were encased with expensive looking boots. Even though Sadie was a self-made business woman she distinctly lacked confidence. Observing how the gathering mingled and carried themselves she began to feel even more than she had done previously that she didn't belong in this world.

Warwick's parents had been welcoming enough but she had foolishly felt very self-conscious with every exaggerated vowel that had left her mouth owing to her Birmingham accent. Just like Warwick, his family and ever-present house guests had all spoken so eloquently and what she considered to be 'properly'.

Mealtimes had also been a chore. Sadie hadn't even realised until now that there was an etiquette for handling cutlery in line with the order of dishes as they arrived. Working from the outside for starters and so forth was a whole new experience for our Brummie girl. She had raised a laugh amongst her hosts by using what she had presumed just to be her fork of choice, not realising that it had been reserved for a specific part of the meal. She hoped that the dimmed light had shielded her blushes.

Luckily the starter had been asparagus based whilst the main had been fresh salmon and vegetables. She hadn't needed to explain that she was a pescatarian or embarrassingly leave masses of untouched meat on the side of her plate.

Yet nevertheless, Sadie had enjoyed her weekend. How could she not in such luxurious surroundings and as usual Warwick had been lovely to her. One thing with him being raised this way was his ability to behave precisely like a gentleman.

But as she watched out of the window, all of a sudden, she really did feel like she didn't belong here. Sadie had noticed that along with the expensive country attire they were covered in from head to toe, each member of the party were also holding a gun. This could only mean one thing. One thing that went entirely against all of her core values. They were going on a hunt.

Just then a knock came on the door. Sadie managed a smile, she knew it must be Warwick.

"You may enter, kind sir." But Sadie's smile soon diminished when she saw Warwick enter the room wearing a similar get-up and a rifle sloped over his shoulder.

"Ahh, you've spotted the crowd outside the window. I wanted it to be a surprise. I've told Father that we will catch them up, which will give you time to get ready. I have a pair of mother's boots that you can borrow and how's this…" Warwick brought his hand from behind his back. "Ta-dah! Your very own deerstalker hat."

Sadie felt her stomach uncomfortably flip. "That's very sweet Warwick, but I'm sorry, I don't really want to go."

Warwick's face dropped with genuine disappointment. "Why not? I thought you'd love going on your very first shooting."

"Is it clay pigeon shooting?"

Warwick laughed, almost mockingly. "Of course not. You're in the country now my dear, we shoot the real thing. Pheasants, pigeons, rabbits, squirrels, even deer if we're lucky. You really should give it a try. I know you won't have experienced hunting before."

"Why's that Warwick, because I'm from such a lower

class than you?"

"That's not what I meant, Sadie."

"Look Warwick, you're right, I've never been shooting before but not because of my class. I simply don't believe in killing animals."

"But it's such fun and you get to eat what you've killed most of the time."

"Warwick, I'm sorry. I know you saw this as a surprise for me but I don't ever want to kill an animal and I don't ever want to eat an animal either. I'm a pescatarian."

"So, you'd go fishing with me then?"

"Funny."

"You can't know that you don't like shooting until you've tried it. You'll love it, it's impossible not to. The adrenaline rushes through your body as you take aim at your target and all of a sudden you feel this enormous sense of power knowing that an animal's life is totally in your hands and it becomes your choice and your choice alone if they live or die." Warwick was almost salivating as he spoke his slow and deliberate words. "And when you pull the trigger, then hear the gunshot and the surrounding birds fly away with fright and confusion while you watch the very prey that you've carefully stalked fall to the floor, the feeling of exhilaration at that precise moment is beyond compare. You will never ever feel so in control of anything again at that very moment when you have chosen to extinguish life."

Warwick's words seemed callous and Sadie was unnerved. He obviously enjoyed killing a creature a bit too much for her liking. This was not the Warwick she'd grown fond of. The problem was she had perhaps even begun to fall in love with him.

"Warwick, do you know how cruel that all sounds?"

Warwick turned, raising his voice to her for the first time ever and displaying an air of impatience that had been alien to their relationship up until this point. "Cruel? Cruel? Life is all about survival of the fittest, don't you get that? That's what the rules are for all of us. There's no point trying to ignore it. Only the strong survive. Do-gooders like you Sadie never live in the real world. You refuse to face up to reality with all your ideology of caring and equality. How can a pheasant deserve the same respect as a human if it is stupid enough to be tracked and killed so easily? Tell me, can a squirrel split the atom or perform life-saving surgery? Can a deer drive a car or fly a plane? The superior are meant to survive, that's just how the world is."

"But you do have a choice, Warwick. You could choose not to kill animals and still have intellectual superiority. In fact, as you are able to make that very choice and not exercise barbarity you would display a true sense of intelligence."

"And why would I want to stop doing something that I enjoy?"

"How can you enjoy killing another living thing?"

"Because when you are victorious in any situation it makes you feel good. You can't deny that, Sadie."

"Killing something isn't a sign of victory, you moron."

An awkward silence filled the room as tempers frayed. Then a sinister smile slowly began to spread across Warwick's face.

"I never did tell you why I got kicked out of Oxford, did I, Sadie?"

Sadie now began to feel very vulnerable. "No, you didn't."

Warwick smiled a further smile that somehow suddenly changed his whole persona. "Well it's about time you knew, but first I want to explore your misplaced notion of right and wrong."

"Don't you try and psycho-analyse me, Warwick. I know that you think you're better than me but you're not."

"Oh, but I am better than you Sadie, and I'm not talking about anything to do with comparing our class. Tell me, is being truthful a good thing?"

"Yes, I believe it is."

"Well. I'm being truthful when I tell you I want to kill animals. I enjoy it, I see nothing wrong with it and many people the world over agree with me. If you have a licence then hunting animals is perfectly accepted in our society. Is this true?"

"It's accepted, but I don't agree with it."

"But you must agree with me, technically because I have the correct permits I'm doing nothing wrong by shooting dead a woodland animal."

"Technically and morally you're a dick."

"So, tell me Sadie, have you never, ever felt like killing someone? Has anyone ever hurt you so much that you've wanted them dead? A bully at school perhaps?"

"Sure, I've felt like I want people dead but I've never had the inclination to make it happen."

"So, I too have had this feeling but remember what I said about being truthful. Well, I was true to my feelings and I tried to make it happen."

"At Oxford?"

"At Oxford. I shared my accommodation with another boy, his name was Tarquin Small. Small was a nasty piece of work but he was as popular as a pile of horse shit is to a swarm of bluebottles. He thought it prudent to enhance his population at my expense. Our peers found it extremely amusing that he would play these never-ending tricks on me. Once, he got me drunk until I passed out, pretending to be my best friend, only to place my hand in cold water until I pissed myself whilst I slept. The photo of me lying in a pool of pee was taken and uploaded on social media here, there and everywhere. I was the joke of Oxford Uni whilst Tarquin was everyone's entertaining best friend. Another time he put chilli powder in my shampoo. My eyes burned like hell for hours. There are many more stories but are you starting to get the picture?"

"Yeah, Tarquin was an arsehole. Couldn't you tell anyone?"

"What would it have achieved? Who could I tell?"

"The lecturers, teachers or whatever they are called."

"They all loved him more than the students. It was hopeless for me so the power of the gun was all that I could turn to."

"You shot him?"

"Not quite. Although he would have deserved it. But it suddenly occurred to me that the only time I really ever feel in total control of anything is when I'm holding a gun and pointing it at a living target. So, after the Christmas semester, I returned to Uni with my trusty hunting gun and pointed it right at Tarquin fucking Small until I made *him* piss himself this time. I instructed him to stand on a chair naked whilst he spoke into a camera admitting to the world that he was a spiteful dickhead and that he was very sorry for the way that he had treated me. Let me tell you, Sadie, having this power over him was the best thing I could have ever hoped for so keeping him alive and toying with him became even more gratifying than extinguishing his pathetic life. So actually, killing something or someone is not the worst thing you can do Sadie, keeping them alive can be far worse. The trouble is he grassed me up. Can you believe it? The audacity of him running to tell tales after all the things that he had done to me. And that was it. Oxford University kicked me out there and then."

"So, you wouldn't kill a human then?"

"Never say never, Sadie. The circumstances may be right to kill a human. In Tarquin's case killing him was too good for him. He needed to suffer and I'm sure to this day his ego has never recovered."

Sadie felt sick. "How can it ever be right to kill a human?"

"Some humans deserve death much more than animals do. I accept your theory that animals are innocent Sadie, but humans are very rarely innocent."

"That doesn't mean they have to die."

"I think some do, if they deserve it. It's survival of the

fittest remember."

"You're crazy."

"No, I'm not. You just can't get your tiny little mind around it all. You can't comprehend what I'm telling you. What if I told you that being killed can even benefit someone?"

"How can being killed ever benefit anyone?"

"Think about it, Sadie. Many people have been assassinated over the years. JFK, Martin Luther King, Gandhi, Che Guevara the list goes on. Yet the actual intended purpose of the assassination never works. These people are killed in an attempt to silence their message but in reality, their cause lives on and on and even becomes augmented, gathering size and pace as their death provides a sharper focus like a runaway snowball. So, killing them actually results in benefiting them."

"None of those people you mentioned should have had to die for their beliefs."

"But you can't deny that their cause prospered after being shot dead. There hasn't been a killing like that for some time and think about it, who is around these days who anyone actually listens too? You know with my gun I could kill a human and do them a massive favour. Kill two birds with one stone so to speak." Warwick actually began to cackle.

"Do you have anyone in mind?"

"I think there is a particular person who wants to die so I could help them do it and at the same time, we could both have eternal fame. People noticed me when I pointed a gun at someone as insignificant as Tarquin Small, imagine how I'd be noticed if I actually did kill someone of worth. Look at the shootings of John Lennon and JFK for instance. The killers are as famous as their victims. Everyone has heard of Lee Harvey Oswald and Mark David Chapman. Both men and more like them are key pointers in history. Their actions had a dramatic impact that changed their previous anonymity. They made a stark difference to the world, it cannot be denied. Perhaps it's time the world knew of Warwick Stansfield, the man famous for…"

"Famous for killing who Warwick? Who is this person you think wants to die?"

Warwick smiled, cocked his gun and pointed it at Sadie. "It's funny how people take notice of someone holding a gun."

Sadie had never felt so scared and her desperate panicking served to amuse her disturbed boyfriend as he continued to point his gun. "Not me, Warwick, not me. I don't want to die. How would killing me achieve anything? How would killing a Birmingham Coffee shop owner help you?"

Sadie closed her eyes and shivered deep within her core, agonisingly waiting for the end of her life to transpire.

CHAPTER 10
THE CHANCE MEETING

Ever since the discovery that his friend William Chamberlain possessed the powers of telekinesis, Judd Stone had kept an open mind on most things. It hadn't therefore taken much for him to buy into the notion of numerology. The idea that a number could prominently feature in the recurrence of coincidental events fascinated him profoundly.

And in his moments of deep thought, Judd had often considered if there actually was such a thing as simple coincidence. Instead, he tended to believe that the coming together of connections, no matter how random the derision, were destined to be linked through the workings of supernatural powers as part of the mapping out of a certain unconscious yet necessary conclusion.

Naturally then when Judd came across Sadie White for the first time he saw it as a sign that any doubts he had of pursuing the protection of Phoenix Easter needed to be put to rest once and for all. He didn't view himself as someone special or 'the chosen one' or anything like that, but he did realise that he did have a mission to fulfil.

Phoenix Easter needed to be saved from harm and he was the most palpable person to do it. And Sadie White helped him to understand this.

Judd was on the train travelling back to Birmingham following a visit to William and his partner Crystal. William and Crystal had moved home to be closer to their place of scientific and paranormal research, and in tandem to paying his friends a social visit, Judd had picked the well-educated brain of Crystal on the subject of numerology.

As Sadie White looked out of the train window, Judd had grown more and more concerned as he watched the girl bravely trying hard to fight back the tears. Something or someone had clearly upset her and Judd could stand it no longer. The time of travel had fortunately resulted in a sparsely populated carriage and the girl had been sitting alone at a table built for four passengers. That was until Judd sat opposite her.

"Forgive me, I couldn't help noticing that you seem to be upset about something. Feel free to tell me to mind my own business but I don't like to see a damsel in distress."

"Mind your own business."

"Fair enough. I wasn't hitting on you, honest. Clearly, I'm old enough to be your dad, or perhaps an older brother. Yeah, I prefer older brother." Judd smiled. "I was just concerned that's all. I'll return to my previous seat and leave you be. I didn't mean to be invasive."

As Judd stood up Sadie spoke. "Sorry, I didn't mean to be rude. I've just had a bit of a shock today that's all."

"I'm a good listener," Judd said as he sat back down and this time Sadie didn't seem to mind.

"I'm Judd," he said offering his hand.

"Sadie."

The pair amicably shook hands.

"Pleased to meet you, Sadie. So, what's this shock you've had?"

"Believe me you wouldn't want to know, and if I told you you'd think I was crazy anyhow."

"You reckon? I used to be a detective, there's not much that could surprise me, believe me. And I learnt a long time ago when I'm being had. I doubt you'd be crying for no good reason so come on, try me."

"You used to be a detective? Really?"

"Really."

"Why used to be?"

"I got sacked. Someone assisted in me losing the love of my life and although I should have known better I beat them to a pulp."

"Perhaps they deserved it."

"Not really. They were only doing their job."

"But no-one fucks with you, right?"

"Something like that, I guess."

"So, what was their job?"

"The guy was a private investigator, and clearly he was good at it too because he was able to prove to my girlfriend that I was cheating on her. So, how's that? I was a detective and someone out-detected me!"

"You sound like a really nice guy – not."

"I did my time, Sadie for beating up that guy. And now I'm unemployed, kind of anyhow, and I have no girl., but I know it was all my own fault. I've been to hell and back which perhaps puts me in a good place to be able to help you."

"You know what I think Judd."

"What?"

"You're a rough diamond. You're actually a bit of a gentleman really, even though you're capable of beating the shit out of someone. Mind you I was wrong about the last person I thought was a gentleman, perhaps I'm not such a good judge of character after all."

"And this guy you were wrong about, he's the fool that's made you cry?"

"Yeah but it's not what you think. This isn't just a lover's tiff. Far from it."

"Well look, if I tell you what I've been up to the last

few hours it may help you open up to me."

"Ok."

"I've been to see two of my closest friends, and both these friends can do special things. One can make things move without touching them and the other can talk to dead people. So, I'm sure that whatever you have to tell me isn't going to sound as far out as any of that now is it?"

"Probably not. Actually, you used to be a detective you say? You may be a good person to speak to. Perhaps?"

"You won't know 'til you try, and you're still sitting there after what I've just told you so that's a good sign."

"I still don't know if you'd believe me. It's pretty far out."

"Okay. I see you have your phone with you. Search on the web for Judd Stone and The Crucifier."

Sadie looked a little confused but she did what Judd had was asked of her.

At first, her face didn't show any particular emotion but every now and then she'd look up from reading about the dramatic events of Judd's arrest of the serial killer known as The Crucifier. As the words unfurled she went on to learn how Judd had also brought to justice Marlon Howell, the disgraced former England football manager who had a habit of raping women."

"Wow, Judd. So, you're a bit of a hero by all accounts. You look quite good in this picture too, Judd."

"Flattery will get you everywhere. I guess I am a rough diamond, Sadie. The important thing is you can trust me."

"You know what? I think I can. Ok, I'll tell you, but it'll sound weird."

"Go for it."

"Well, this guy who I thought was a gentleman. It turns out he's far from it and is actually obsessed with guns and death."

"Sounds a nice guy. He's your boyfriend?"

"Was."

"Well, that's a good start already if you've kicked him

into touch. Did this jerk hurt you?" Judd noticed Sadie's eyes begin to fill up again.

"I thought he was going to kill me."

"What did he do?"

"He pointed a gun at my face and I could see in his eyes that he was excited by the fear that he created in me. He was so in control of me at that moment in time I could tell that he thought he had the power of a king. It was really scary."

"But he didn't hurt you?"

"Not physically. He started to slowly pull the trigger and then at the last moment, he moved the gun from my face. I felt the bullet whizz over my shoulder and then a chunk of plaster fell from the ceiling with the impact."

"What a psycho. Then what?"

"He began to laugh. Then he told me not to worry because he could never hurt me because he loved me. He had a funny way of showing it I'd say but he insisted that he did and he was just showing me how fantastic it is to be so in control of a situation.

"He told me that with a gun in your hand you can have anything you want. Then he really gave me the creeps. He went on to say that by killing the right person you can even achieve fame. He informed me about all these assassinations that had happened and how the shooter had gained global recognition. I didn't really want to listen, I just wanted to run out of there and keep on running but I was literally too afraid to move. I hate to admit it but the bastard did indeed have total control over me."

"So, he spoke about the killing of John Lennon for example?"

"Yeah, he did."

"That murder is one that's very close to my heart. I'm a huge Lennon fan, but what people like your boyfriend, erm ex-boyfriend don't understand is that yes, the killers achieve the fame but what's great about creating a mammoth legacy of hatred. Mark David Chapman, the killer of John Lennon, is loathed by millions upon millions of people. And what he actually achieved was to strengthen the love for John Lennon. Whereas, the motive for which they kill is never achieved."

"It's frightening isn't it that some people are so warped that they doggedly believe their own take on things without even a hint of flexibility."

"Yeah, it is. So how did you get away?"

"I literally had to wait until the rest of his family were back in the house and for him to eventually go to the toilet. Let me tell you, I put on an Oscar-winning performance pretending to be the perfect girlfriend and telling him I understood and agreed with exactly what he was telling me, even though I didn't of course. So, he went the loo, and luckily, he had a shower afterwards which brought me some valuable time. He had an obsession with keeping clean too. He could shower two or three times a day. I announced to his parents that they needed to speak with Warwick, that's his name, and I made my excuses and left. I told them that I needed to get a taxi into town, alone, as I wanted to purchase a gift as a thank you for making me so welcome in their home for the weekend. They said there was no need but under the circumstances, I became very insistent and I left. Unbeknown to them I had no intention of returning."

"Wow, well thought through but it sounds like you had a lucky escape. Look don't worry, I still have mates in the force. If this Warwick has an unhealthy interest in guns I can get him looked at."

"I see little point. I went to the local police before going to the train station. They checked their records and as Warwick and the members of his family had legitimate licenses for guns they said there wasn't anything to be alarmed about. When I told them what he'd done they just laughed at me and didn't take me seriously. They said no-one had been hurt and I had not actually been threatened so there was no crime to investigate."

"I may have more influence, Sadie."

"What really frightened me is what he said about someone I really admire. He said he knew of a way to make them eternally famous while making myself famous and I could also be the catalyst to make them forever young. He said if I was the one to hold the gun I could feel what it was like to have that ultimate moment of control and change the course of history forever. He said I would have an unrivalled amount of power literally at my fingertips. What worries me is that although I don't want the power he speaks of what if he does?"

Judd became concerned. Hooked but concerned. "He said this person can become eternally famous and forever young? Did forever young mean forever 27 do you know? As in joining the 27 club?"

Sadie thought hard for a moment. "Come to think of it, he did mention the 27 club."

"This person who you admire. The same person who appears to be in danger. Is this person Phoenix Easter by any chance?"

"Yes, it is. I'm a huge fan of Phoenix."

"Tell me, Sadie, do you believe in coincidence?"

CHAPTER 11
THE PRIVATE INVESTIGATOR

Fate, or maybe something else, had provided Judd with a prime suspect in the potential demise of Phoenix Easter. However, Judd had been around long enough to realise that a good investigator doesn't put all their eggs in one basket so he decided to cast his net a little wider to investigate the state of affairs that Ben Francis had tasked him with.

But Judd was no longer a serving detective, instead, he had by all accounts evolved to become an investigator with an underpinning glowing reference provided by DSI Ben Francis. So, when Judd had assessed his position only a few days earlier he made it official. Judd Stone Private Investigator had been born.

Judd had found his decision to be quite an ironic one considering how he had found himself to be in this situation, but he needed a job. No, it was more than that. He needed a definite purpose. A reason to get up in the morning. So, Judd had decided to formalise the work that Ben was funding and in addition advertise his services to provide private investigations. Besides, he simply just liked the sound of Judd Stone P.I. Judd had been hooked on viewing the light-hearted American series Magnum P.I during the 1980s, though he was going to draw the line at growing the trademark Tom Selleck moustache!

It had also crossed Judd's mind that implementing investigations completely on his own terms could be a very attractive proposition compared to constantly having to wrestle with the previous etiquette of the police force. Judd realised this meant his working outside of any rules which for Judd naturally made the prospect even more attractive.

And apart from Thomas Magnum, the most famous fictional PI had surely been Sherlock Holmes – a series of stories he had always enjoyed reading. The adventures of both men had inspired Judd to fully become accustomed to the romantic notion of being a Private Investigator. Suddenly it occurred to him that this had perhaps always been his destiny. Judd's head had been swimming with all the positive thoughts of clichés such as 'as one door closes another one opens' and perhaps he was finally about to truly embark upon 'living the dream'.

Judd had decided to run his investigations from his Rotunda home, so his apartment began to double up as an office. This negated any worries regarding overheads.

At the moment he was researching, for the umpteenth time, the essence of the 27 club to determine if there was any guiding light to suggest where the danger to Phoenix Easter was destined to strike. During his explorations, it occurred to him that the trends contributing to the deaths involved with the members of the 27 club suggested that the person most likely to cause harm to Phoenix Easter was actually Phoenix herself! Many of the 27 Club members had significantly contributed to their own deaths through their self-destructive approach to drugs or alcohol. And Phoenix Easter had a firm reputation for heavily indulging in both.

So, Judd currently had two prime suspects. Warwick

Stansfield and Phoenix Easter!

Judd hadn't ruled out the possibility of a conspiracy theory or two either leading to the deaths of these talented people at the tender age of 27, but that was for another day. His mind couldn't cope with the bigger questions just yet and he wanted to concentrate on the basic facts for now.

Just then the 'office' phone rang. Judd had now had a distinct landline installed for his new line of work, keeping it separate from his domestic line.

"Hello, JS Private Investigation services. How can I help you?" Judd felt smug believing that the title of his new occupation sounded really good as he said it out loud for the first time.

"I want you to catch my cheating bastard husband with his pants down and I'm willing to pay extra if you chop off his cock."

"Certainly Madam," replied Judd, thinking to himself that apart from the exciting but challenging prevention of the death of Phoenix Easter, now that he was officially a PI was the investigating of extra-marital affairs all that he had to look forward to in reality?

So much for living the dream!

CHAPTER 12
THE SIEGE

Sadie's coffee business was doing very well of late, so much so she had recruited Justin Corrigan on Judd's recommendation. The young apprentice had proved to be a willing and industrious addition to the small but perfectly formed team of three which still included best pal, Jolie. And the employment meant that Justin was bringing in a regular and legitimate wage which prevented his dear old nana from having to worry about what financial mess he was going to get himself into next.

Today had been a good day for takings. It was mid-morning and currently, there was the typical daily flow of students that arrived for their ritualistic fix of coffee along with some wider-ranging customers such as the visiting grand-parents of a Drama and Theatre Arts student who were occupying the space in the cute little alcove which Sadie had themed with Hollywood legends.

Unfortunately, though the pleasantries of the day were soon to be compromised - as well as the state of Sadie's ceiling!

Following the gunshot into the air the quintessential

English voice spoke amongst the manic screams and disbelieving gasps.

"It pleases me that I have your attention. As you can see this thing I'm holding is real and it's clear that I'm not here to mess around." The gunman then pointed his gun at the group of stunned students who were sat nearest the door and instructed them to stand up and begin an orderly queue in front of the coffee shop counter. The shaken students dutifully complied and the gunman ensured that the remainder of terrified customers followed suit.

Justin assessed the situation and realised that he and Jolie were standing out of sight behind the gunman with Sadie within range from the corner of his eye – deliberately it would seem. Justin fancied his chances and made his move but the gunman turned on a sixpence and cocked the trigger before speaking once more in that posh accent of his. "You can try and be a hero if you wish but nothing will give me greater pleasure than actually making you zero. So, what's it to be?"

Justin took a step back, frustrated and a little scared at the same time.

"Now you and little Miss Pretty here can also go and join the back of the queue."

"What about Sadie?"

"She's staying right where she is. Now move it – keep things nice and slow - and don't try anything remotely gallant."

Justin and Jolie did as they were told and moved to the back of the queue.

Now that she was isolated from the crowd, the gunman turned his entire attention onto Sadie. "I'm doing all of this for you, Sadie. This is how much you mean to me. Just look at the lengths I am willing to go to just to be able to speak with you. I just want to talk and sort things out but you've been ignoring my calls and texts so what else am I meant to do? This way I know you're going to listen to me and then it'll all be alright."

"How can this ever be alright?" answered Sadie.

The gunman was perturbed by Sadie's challenge but aimed his anger towards the line of people. Markedly pointing his gun at them he snapped: "Now all of you lot sit on the floor and cross your legs."

Naturally, the queue of people obeyed the order. However, once they were seated the gunman was amazed to discover that there was one customer who hadn't complied with his instructions. This guy had incredulously remained sitting at a table reading his paper and seemed totally oblivious to the hostage situation that was unfolding before him.

"Hey, you. Are you on some type of a death wish? Didn't you hear me? Get in line with all these others. Now!"

Judd never broke eye contact from his newspaper as he calmly answered the gunman. "Not just now mate if it's all the same to you. I'm just checking out the sports pages. You carry on though, don't mind me."

"Are you crazy? I've got a loaded gun here."

"I'm aware of that, I couldn't help but notice the damage that you caused to the ceiling with your loaded gun. Never mind, though. Shit happens, huh."

The gunman was exasperated. "I'm going to count to three and if you haven't moved to join the line of people I'm going to blow your fucking head off."

Judd just shrugged and carried on reading his newspaper.

"1."

There was no sign of Judd standing up to join the queue.

"2."

Still nothing except the sound and sight of turning pages.

"I'm not joking mister. Get the fuck up."

"You're not going to pull that trigger Warwick, you're smarter than that."

"How do you know my name?"

"That's for me to know and for you to never find out if you pull that trigger."

Warwick hadn't been expecting this little situation to have developed and in a state of bewilderment, he wasn't entirely sure how to react. "Look, don't fuck with me, mister. I'm warning you."

Judd decided to calmly fold away his newspaper before swivelling his chair in order to face Warwick for the first time.

"You're new at this game aren't you, Warwick?"

"What makes you say that?"

"Well while we've been having our cosy little chat here, who's to say that one of these delightful people that you have sitting on the floor haven't already managed to relay a message to the emergency services? The first rule of thumb for any hostage situation, Warwick. You, the aggressor I guess we could call you, should confiscate all of the mobile phones from your hostages. And then get them to place their hands on their heads so they can't do anything that could compromise your intentions."

"I was just about to do all of that but then I spotted you dicking about didn't I?" lied Warwick, not wanting to appear incompetent. He pointed the gun down the line of seated people. "You lot, slowly empty your pockets and throw your mobile phones out in front of you and then place your hands on your heads. And no funny business."

Once again, the hostages complied.

"There you are, Warwick. Now you have some control of the hostages. The thing is what is it that you want to actually gain from this situation?"

"I want to talk to Sadie; the hostages are just caught up in all of this."

"Oh, I see, they're just in the wrong place at the wrong time?"

"Exactly."

"So, let them go."

"What?"

"Let them go. If you never wanted any hostages in the first place let them go."

"But if I let them go they'll go and talk to the authorities and this place will be surrounded by police. I can't allow that to happen."

Judd managed to project a persona of genuine concern for Warwick. "Ok, I understand. But they are innocent in all of this. Wait, I have an idea. Why not take them into a back room and lock them in there. That way they are out of harm's way and more importantly they can't listen in to whatever it is that's so important that you need to speak with Sadie about."

Judd and Warwick exchanged a stare. Warwick hadn't contemplated this level of engagement from one of the inevitable bystanders and was ducking in and out of trusting the stranger before him. Confused and now pretty much going on auto-pilot he finally spoke. "Ok, you. The hero," he said pointing his gun towards Justin. "Come here."

Justin stood up and walked towards Warwick. "You work here so tell me, do you have a room with a lock?"

"Yes," replied Justin. "We have a room out of sight from the customers where we take our lunch break."

"Ok, now pay attention, hero. This gun is going to be pointed on you at all times so don't try anything foolish. Lead these people into the room you speak of, lock the door and then come back and join me, Sadie and whoever this guy is."

"How rude of me, I should have introduced myself earlier. My name's Judd."

"I'm not stupid, Judd. I'll work out soon enough why you're pretending to help me?"

"I'm just a helpful kind of a guy, Warwick."

Warwick returned his attention to Justin. "Do it now."

It took a couple of minutes for the operation to be finalised which resulted in Warwick and his gun overseeing the arrangements of Judd, Justin and Sadie.

"Ok, you two chaps go and sit down the far end of the cafe. I need to speak with my girlfriend."

"I'm not your girlfriend anymore, Warwick."

Warwick sharply pointed the gun at Sadie which caused her to flinch.

Judd discreetly intervened once again to diminish the intense focus on Sadie. "Justin, do as the nice man says while I make us a coffee. You don't mind if I just make Justin and I a cup of coffee do you, Warwick? You carry on speaking with Sadie, don't mind me. You won't even know I'm there."

Once again Warwick didn't quite know how to react as Judd matter-of-factly moved behind the counter and started working at the coffee machine.

Unanswered questions began to race through Warwick's head. Was this guy, Judd, some kind of psycho? Why on earth was he not in the least bit scared of a man with a gun? And how the fuck does this guy know my name?

Warwick kept the gun pointed at Sadie.

In truth, Judd's unorthodox behaviour was compromising Warwick's intent to be in total control, something which he usually felt when he was holding a gun. Judd was uncomfortably bucking the trend and Warwick was struggling to cope as he didn't have anywhere near a grip on the situation like he expected.

"Make it quick, Judd, and while you're at it you can tell me how you know who I am. Can you read minds or something?"

"No Warwick, but believe it or not I do know a man who can, although that's not for discussion now. Just a lucky guess, that's all. You see I was speaking with Sadie one day and she told me about how she had fallen for this posh kid who liked guns probably more than he liked her. When you came in here brandishing that firearm about and speaking in a posh-boy accent I kinda figured who you were. Now the thing is you're also proving her point at the moment, aren't you?"

"Huh?"

"Well, you clearly like guns more than you like Sadie."

"That's bullshit."

"Ok, I believe you but you use guns to get what you want, Warwick. That's no way to win a girl over is it now? You're more likely to scare her off than win her love for you. By the way, do you want a coffee?"

"Err no thanks."

"And what if she still refuses to get back with you after your little chat, what then?"

"Then I'll kill her. If I can't have her then nobody can."

Sadie let out a small scream.

"Warwick, mate you've got this all wrong. The girl who you love shouldn't feel the bullet from your gun. Killing Sadie's not the answer. You can kill a coffee shop proprietor if you want but if you're gonna do it why not think big, let's say someone famous – someone like Phoenix Easter, perhaps. You need to at least make the killing worthwhile then that way you're going to impress Sadie too. Sadie lives and you win her over. Simple."

"I've already thought about that. I told Sadie that we could kill Phoenix Easter together and in doing so we would be famous forever. It would force people to take notice of us."

"That's more like it. Killing Sadie will get you a thirty-year stretch and for what? You wouldn't have your girlfriend anymore. Killing someone famous is much more worthwhile. You could really make a name for yourself."

"But it means nothing if that's not what Sadie wants. That's why I need to talk to her." Warwick switched his focus heavily on Sadie. "Sadie, I love you. I need you to be with me."

"That sounds wonderful, Warwick. But I just need you to put that gun away. You're scaring me."

Good girl thought Judd, keep massaging the dickhead's

ego.

"I told you I could make you famous by killing Phoenix. I thought you understood but then you ran away from me."

"I don't want Phoenix dead, Warwick. I like her music so why would I want that to end?"

"Because she would be forever young and her music would take on a new meaning. And it would be you and I that enabled that to happen. The world would owe us a debt that could never be paid. If we were to do it together we would be famous beyond words and look what we would have done for her career. We will make her and her music timeless.

"And at that very moment when you are holding the trigger and it is your choice that someone so powerful is at your mercy and it is only you that has the ability to change the face of history what greater feeling can there be? To literally have the control of history in the palm of your hand. It's the greatest gift I could give to you and to Phoenix."

"The greatest gift is to let her live."

"I understand how you feel, Sadie. I've thought a lot about why you went away and obviously the thought of killing someone scared you. But I know that killing someone can be a good thing and I only ever feel in control when I have a gun in my hand. Now if you don't want to implement that possibility and you also choose not to be with me then no-one is going to have you, it's as simple as that. I need to be in control of the situation, if it's not with Phoenix then it's got to be with you." Warwick pointed the gun squarely at Sadie once again.

Things had now taken an unexpected turn and Judd knew he had to think fast.

"No Warwick, how will you serving time for killing the woman you love ever help you?"

"I don't plan to do time, Judd. Once I have killed Sadie then I will take my own life. If we can't achieve great things together in life then we'll be together in death."

"But she does want to be with you. Don't you Sadie?"

"Stop trying to mess with my mind, Judd," said Warwick.

"Warwick, it's true. I do want to be with you. I just don't like the guns being involved."

"I wish I could believe you, Sadie. There's only one way we are going to be together. I know that now."

Judd intervened. "Oh, this is getting boring now. Can I just take these coffees down to Justin and I'll let you get on with whatever you're thinking of doing, Warwick?"

Judd took hold of the coffees and incredulously walked directly in-between the line of sight between Warwick and Sadie, once again presenting Warwick with a level of confusion of how to react to such adverse behaviour by Judd considering the circumstances.

For a split second as Judd walked past, Warwick pulled the gun back from taking aim and that split second was enough for Judd to throw the two scorching cups of water into the gunman's face. Warwick screamed with pain and automatically pulled his hands to his burning face. He was still holding the gun but Judd grabbed at the hand that was holding it and with all his yester-years of combat training was able to easily take it from the assailant.

Warwick managed to open his eyes following the scolding only to find Judd Stone looking down the barrel of a gun at him. "Don't even think about it Warwick or I won't hesitate to unload this little beauty into your sad little body."

"He means it, Warwick," said Sadie.

Suddenly the noise of sirens could be heard entering the grounds of the university.

"Ahh, it looks as though someone did get a message to the police, after all, Warwick. You really are such an amateur. It'll be nice for me to catch up with some old friends as I hand you over to them.

"Oh, and say goodbye to Sadie on your way out.

Forever."

CHAPTER 13
THE FLAWED GENIUS

Phoenix Easter sang out the last note of her self-penned track and promptly took a swig from her bottle of Bourbon whisky. "So how was that?" she slurred into the microphone.

"That was great, Phoenix, really great," said Blaze the well-renowned record producer being a little too diplomatic. "But perfection isn't an instant thing, we'll go again tomorrow…when you're sober." Phoenix had been spared hearing Blaze's final three words as he muted the conversation at the flick of a button and prevented them from entering her earphones. However, a conversation continued outside of Phoenix's hearing with Neima, her frustrated manager.

"That was such a shit vocal. She was so below-par. She can hardly stand up in there. I don't know what to do with her sometimes."

"I know it's frustrating Neima, but history tells us that the recording artists who have a little craziness in their make-up are the ones that also provide us with musical genius."

"I know, I know but I just worry for her safety. She's got that dickhead of a boyfriend feeding her drugs left, right and centre on top of all the booze that she eagerly self-procures. I'm genuinely worried that she won't make it to her 27th birthday but she just isn't prepared to listen to me. I really don't know how to help her anymore."

"Hey, you do a great job managing Phoenix, Neima, which I know isn't easy. No one could do the job better than you do," Blaze was being one-hundred percent genuine this time.

"Thanks, Blaze. I don't ever want to let her down. Come on, give Phoenix the nod, we'll go again in the morning if her hangover isn't too harsh."

Blaze mastered the controls in order to make a connection with the superstar, but all they heard coming from the vocal booth was the sound of Phoenix snoring.

CHAPTER 14
THE TRAP

"I'm very sorry to have to tell you Mrs. Abbey that I can confirm that your husband is indeed having an affair."

"I knew it, the cheating bastard. Over twenty years of marriage and he does this to me."

Since the arrest of Warwick Stansfield, the investigation into Phoenix Easter becoming the next member of the 27 club no longer seemed as significant for Judd, and as predicted much of his work as a private investigator had hinged on the continual likelihood of people engaging in extra-marital affairs.

Judd produced an A4 sized brown envelope and proceeded to show Loretta Abbey a series of photographs showing her husband in various clinches of passion with a woman who Loretta Abbey knew very well.

"It can't be?" she said in disbelief. "Shona is meant to be my best friend. She was my chief bridesmaid for Christ's sake. The bitch, I'll kill her. I'll fucking kill her. And I'll fucking kill him."

"I have further evidence to prove that your husband has been seeing Miss Kyle for at least the past ten years. I really am very sorry to confirm your suspicions, Mrs. Abbey and to reveal the unlikely source at the heart of this unfortunate matter. I've brought you here today because without fail the two of them will ritualistically leave the exit of this hotel within the next half-an-hour."

"No wonder the cow never married, she had my no-good arsehole of a husband on bloody tap! How could I have been so stupid? The two people I trusted the most in the whole wide world end up doing this to me."

"Don't blame yourself, Mrs. Abbey. The partner is always the last to know. I know it's a cliché but from my recent experience, it's true. I also have evidence that before, and even during his time seeing your best friend, your husband engaged in casual liaisons with both his secretary and a string of prostitutes."

"So, it seems he is gifted at living up to clichés. Best friends, secretaries and prostitutes. At least he's cheated on Shona too, the daft cow. What did I ever see in that man?"

"I know it's easy for me to say but one of the most important things is not to blame yourself, Mrs. Abbey."

"Please, call me Loretta."

"Ok, Loretta. Thank you. It's a common reaction for the err, victim for want of a better word…"

"No that's what I am, there's no need to sugarcoat any of this. I am a victim."

"When things have sunk in and you've fully digested the facts, it's not uncommon for the victim to start searching their brains with questions as to why this happened. People often wonder could they have done things differently etcetera. I have some specialists I can put you in touch with who can help you come to terms with all this."

"Counsellors?"

"Yes, mainly. Support Groups too."

"It's my fucking soon-to-be ex-husband and best friend who are going to need the help once I've finished with them. He's finally going to be able to utilise that private medical insurance that he's paid in to for all these years. For his sake, let's hope that they can do reconstructive surgery on mangled dicks."

Judd couldn't help but smile at Loretta's colourful language. "Anger, another normal reaction, Loretta."

"Tell me, Judd, you seem like a nice enough guy, but I bet even you have broken a few hearts in your time, haven't you? What is it with you fucking men?"

"I broke one heart for sure, not too long ago as it happens. It was the worst mistake of my life. I honestly can't explain why so many of us do it, Loretta, there's something about having our cake and eating it I guess if we use another cliché here. But I swear to God, if I could have my time again I would never cheat on that special lady ever. I really mean that. Believe me, I pay the price every day. Living with the guilt, the shame and the knowledge that I hurt someone else so badly hurts just as much as having a mangled dick. Yeah, it's true, there are many of us men who are not saints for sure Loretta, however, one overriding observation I have made whilst doing this job and which I've really opened my eyes to is that the human race as a whole can seldom be trusted. I've investigated women cheating on decent loyal husbands who like you didn't deserve the pain. I've also investigated same-sex relationships cheating on one another. It seems a very sad state of affairs for our society doesn't it?"

"I'm sorry but you deserve to be in pain, Judd."

"I know I do. It's been a hard lesson to learn."

"So, you think I should go easy on my husband?"

"That's not my decision to make, Loretta. I just present you with the facts of my investigation for you to decide what to do. However, think about this. Is he capable of genuine remorse or would he only be sorry because he got caught? Does he care more about himself or you? When you've worked that out you'll know what to do."

Not long after Judd had posed his thought-provoking questions, the venom portrayed by Loretta Abbey as she speedily exited the car in the direction of her husband and best friend as they left the hotel provided Judd with his answer.

CHAPTER 15
THE RELAXING CUPPA

"Here you go, one pot of strongly brewed Ceylon tea with two cups to drink from."

"You're joining me, Sadie?" asked Judd hoping that she was. Judd was a regular customer at Sadie's coffee shop these days despite not having anything to do with the university campus.

The on-site wi-fi was a strong connection and enabled his laptop to fire on all cylinders as he found the environment relaxing and productive to undergo his research and investigations.

Today Judd had been able to secure his favourite spot, sitting at the window overlooking the landmark clock tower and its surrounding greenery. He liked Sadie too, she was one of life's sweet souls and her sense of vulnerability, which made her all the more endearing, played into Judd's sub-conscious instinct to protect her. Much of this deep-rooted yearning to protect Sadie had stemmed from the guilt he still felt for the death of his wife at the hands of a twisted ex-con who wanted to teach Judd a lesson, albeit Judd had in turn achieved the ultimate revenge by torturing the 'waste of space' Delroy Whitton before securing his undignified eternal place of rest within a grave of concrete. Judd also still felt responsible for failing to prevent footballer Marlon Howell from raping someone he cared about which led to her eventual suicide. After many years of regret and inward torment, Judd did finally ensure that justice prevailed for Howell's evil actions in dramatic televised circumstances which catapulted Judd into hero status.

Yet no matter how sweet the revenge, Judd would never quite shake the deep-rooted feelings of guilt and failed responsibility which he would always hold. The exercising of revenge is a formidable necessity for Judd, but in truth, he will never completely be free from the demons that plague him concerning the women in his life that he will always believe he has let down.

And of course, cheating on Brooke had done little to ease his conscience either. He knew he was a fool for hurting and losing her.

When was he ever going to learn to stop being so self-destructive?

However, being able to save Sadie White from the clutches of Warwick Stansfield had at least made him feel good about himself for the first time in a long while.

"We're a bit quiet today so I thought I'd join you for an overdue chat. Justin and Jolie can handle any mad rush of customers."

"Great. Shall I be mother?" offered Judd.

"Why not?"

Judd poured the teak-coloured liquid into their respective cups, followed by a splash of milk from the decorative milk jug.

"Sugar?"

"Just half-a-spoon, thanks."

"Half-a-spoon? Is it worth it?"

Sadie chuckled. Judd carefully measured out the half-a-spoon for Sadie and then went on to place the usual four spoonfuls in his own cup of tea.

"That is a lot of sugar, Judd. Yuck!"

Judd smiled. "My friend William used to say the exact same thing when he saw how much sugar I take. It keeps up my energy levels."

"Fair enough. So, how's things?" asked Sadie before placing the cup to her lips and taking a sip of her tea.

"Ok, thanks, Sadie. I was ready for this cuppa though."

"Yeah, we English are quite addicted to the brown coloured nectar, aren't we?"

Judd laughed. "Yeah, we are."

"And some of us sugar too it would seem."

Judd laughed again.

"So, what have you been up to?"

"I'm trying to get my head around this 27 club thing."

"Well, Phoenix shouldn't become a member now Warwick is out of harm's way."

"I wouldn't be so sure, Sadie."

"Oh? I thought it was over?"

"I've been reading this article on Phoenix," said Judd pointing to the screen of his laptop. "She may not need any help from anyone else in ensuring she joins the club. It can all be down to her own making."

"Yeah, her lifestyle is a little wild huh?"

"It certainly is. She makes me look like a monk. And then there are all the conspiracy theories I've been reading."

"Oooh, like what? I love a good conspiracy theory I do."

"Well, one being that these artists actually agreed to die at the age of 27?"

Sadie scrunched up her pretty face in bemusement. "Why would anyone want to do that? And agree with whom?"

"The Devil. They sign a contract with Old Nick to achieve fame and fortune and in return, their soul is handed over to him when they reach the age of 27. It is said that the Blues musician Robert Johnson was the instigator. Well, I guess the Devil was the instigator but Johnson was the original member according to this particular conspiracy theory.

"Wow, go on."

"I don't know how true this theory is myself of course, and if Johnson were alive today I'm sure he would challenge the claims that by all accounts he was by no means a competent guitar player at all originally."

"Really?"

"According to how the legend goes. But nevertheless, Johnson ached to be a recognised force in Blues music. So, apparently, a voice came to him out of nowhere and instructed him that when the clock struck midnight he was to go to the crossroads by a plantation in Mississippi."

"Man, that's scary," Sadie gave a shiver as she became more and more drawn into Judd's story.

"Now if he really did hear a voice at all who's to say Johnson wasn't under the influence of something? Or, perhaps he had simply dreamed it? Anyway, Johnson complied with the instruction and when he reached the crossroads he was met by Satan himself in the guise of a large black man."

"OMG!"

"Johnson had taken his guitar with him to the meeting and the story goes that Satan took it from him, tuned it, played a few riffs and would only return it to him with the understanding that the guitar would undeniably enable him to play guitar at a wondrous level. But the understanding also stretched to accepting the return of the guitar in exchange for his soul."

"What happened?"

"Johnson readily agreed."

"Fuck, no way!"

"Way! Thereafter Robert Leroy Johnson became an instant success in the genre of Blues music, playing guitar with an incredible new-found ability, ironically singing like an angel and writing the kinds of songs that other songwriters could only dream of writing. Then in 1938, he met an untimely death at the tender age of 27."

"What happened to him?"

"Apparently he drank some poisoned whiskey."

"That's rough."

"Yeah, what a horrible way to die, but the story doesn't end there. Certain Satanic high priestesses, albeit whilst remaining anonymous, have since claimed to have insightful knowledge that since Johnson's agreement to take his unusual journey to success, and death, other practitioners in the music industry have followed and have willingly signed up to become a member of the 27 club. By doing this they have been able to secure the fame and fortune that they so desperately desired whilst willingly giving up their soul to Satan in their 27th year."

"Wow, that's a really interesting story. Do you think that's possible, you know that others have followed in Johnson's footsteps?"

"Believe me, I used to be the most cynical person on the planet, but I now know that almost anything's possible. One day I'll introduce you to my friends William and Crystal, they'll be able to open any doors that may be closed in that pretty little mind of yours, Sadie. Crystal, for example, has helped me get my head around some of the numerology theories regarding the 27 club."

"Go on, Judd. Please. I so love all this type of stuff," Sadie took a sip of her tea all wide-eyed.

"Ok, ok. I'm glad that I'm able to keep you entertained. Well in numerology the number 27 when split out and added up i.e. 2 plus 7 presents the number 9, which represents the end of a cycle. One of the few musicians who explicitly believed in numerology and spoke openly about it was John Lennon. Although he didn't die at the age of 27 Lennon believed that he was defined in many ways by the number 9 even predicting that the date of his death would be connected to the number 9. No one can argue that he didn't meet an untimely and tragic death on 8 December 1980 in New York City."

"A tragic death undoubtedly, one of the most shocking and unnecessary in history, but the eighth of December? Doesn't that mean that Lennon got his prediction wrong? Where's the number 9 connection?"

"When Lennon was killed, in UK time back in his native Liverpool the date was 9 December."

"Oh wow, of course it was."

"Furthermore, Lennon's number 9 multiplied by three gives us 27 so it is embedded in the number's cubic ingredients. Also, Lennon's murderer wanted to create an additional chapter of the book *The Catcher In The Rye* which only had twenty-six chapters. The killer whose name was Mark David Chapman at different times of his psyche actually believed he was either Lennon himself or the book's protagonist Holden Caulfield. By killing Lennon he believed he was playing out the twenty-seventh chapter of *The Catcher In The Rye.*"

"That is truly fascinating, and numerology presents yet another whole different theory to the one concerning Robert Johnson."

"There's more yet. If you couple numerology with astrology things get very spooky indeed. The cycle of Saturn, in particular, can cause major changes in life, and of course, a major change can be attributed to the termination of life itself. The Saturn cycle takes about twenty-nine and a bit years, but astrologers most definitely document that the planet's influence in the cycle will surface and register with a person at the age of twenty-seven. The pull of the planet is so forceful coupled with such a compelling influence it is difficult for the affected person to implement any type of control as their destiny unfolds, even if that destiny is a premature death at the age of twenty-seven."

"Bloody hell."

"I can tell that you have an open mind, Sadie. It's

important."

"I do. This kind of thing fascinates me no end."

"And what if I were to tell you that a Fortune Teller told me that I had to save a girl involved in music and at the centre of the threat to her life was the number nine."

"I'd say that I believe you no question, Judd, but surely you've done what was required of you when you got rid of Warwick? We know he was a threat to Phoenix as well as me."

"Maybe, maybe not. The more I research and think and research some more I'm not convinced that Warwick was the only threat. So, you like conspiracy theories then, Sadie?"

"Yeah."

"Do you know the one about the Umbrella Man?"

"That one I don't."

"Well sit back and let me tell you some more stuff."

Judd went on to inform Sadie about the visit he had from Ben and Xanthe. Sadie hung on his every word as he explained about the so-called Umbrella Man's connection with the assassination of JFK and the reappearance of him in photos of members of the 27 club.

Judd then turned his laptop screen to face Sadie. It still had the article about Phoenix displayed and a recent photo of the superstar.

"Look carefully at this photo, Sadie. Bear in mind that Warwick has not been granted bail and has been remanded in custody for a few weeks now. This picture is credited as being only a couple of nights ago when Phoenix started abusing the paparazzi outside a West End nightclub. Two nights ago, there wasn't a drop of rain in London. Tell me, what can you see?"

Sadie scanned the image for only a moment before answering. "Oh my God. There's a man in the picture holding an umbrella."

"Exactly, I think it's time I attempted to pay Miss Easter a visit."

CHAPTER 16
THE DEALER

Judd had targeted the potential locations where access to Phoenix would be most likely. This included the two houses she owned, one situated in North London and the other just outside of Stratford-Upon-Avon, and the remaining locations would usually find Judd gravitating to a choice of nightclub in either London or Birmingham. Additionally, if Phoenix was dwelling in her Warwickshire home, she could frequently be found in any given public house in the centre of Shakespeare's birth town. Ironically, in spite of having a famous resident nearby in which to gain kudos, the strait-laced proprietor of Phoenix's most local country boozer had barred her from the establishment due to her previous drunken behaviour in his pub coupled with her well-documented involvement in drugs.

Judd felt that knocking on the door of either of her two homes was not a viable option, and besides, the lifestyle that Phoenix indulged in meant that obtaining access to such a famous person who was 'out and about' was in truth easier than most, which may help Judd's quest in monitoring her but in turn placed Phoenix in a much more vulnerable position than her peers.

With the most recent controversy surrounding Phoenix taking place in and around a London nightclub Judd almost decided to head to the big smoke, but his investigations had revealed that she was currently in her home city of Birmingham and would, therefore, be attending the Birmingham nightclub that she actually owned which she had called 'The Edge of Heaven'. The distinct advantage of owning your own nightclub of course meant that you couldn't be barred or thrown out!

It was Friday night and The Edge of Heaven was packed with night owls. The club was consistently one of the most popular in Birmingham but the level of attendance would always spike considerably when word got around that Phoenix would be within its walls. However, getting close to the superstar wasn't easy. Phoenix had her own private suite in the club situated behind closed doors, however, a glimpse of Phoenix could potentially be gained if she chose to enter the cordoned-off area designed for VIP guests. This area was situated to the east of the club and Phoenix would utilise it when she wanted to experience a bit more of the club's electric atmosphere.

Following twenty minutes or so queuing outside of the popular nightclub, Judd paid his admission fee and gained access to The Edge of Heaven. He made his way up the stairs and entered the main area of scattered bars and dancefloors. He was in luck. Straight away he could see that Phoenix had opted to utilise the cordoned-off area which meant he could discreetly observe the singer from amongst the camouflage of the nightclubbers.

In truth, he didn't quite know what his next move would be. At this stage, he simply planned to get as close to Phoenix as possible and observe her movements and habits. Identifying the people who surrounded her would also build up his intelligence but he really didn't know what he was actually expecting to happen in connection with Phoenix and the 27 club. Judd had figured that he needed to put in place an operation where he could witness Phoenix and be prepared to act if and when the unexpected happened. Whatever the unexpected may be!

Of course, Judd's initial observations resulted in an easy identification of Phoenix. She was wearing a one-off psychedelic-patterned short jacket over a black bra top which revealed her diamond-studded naval and flat stomach. The natural beauty of her facial features radiated beneath the snugness of her blonde dreadlocks and she simply oozed charisma without even trying.

Many star-struck nightclubbers would stop dead to try and capture a glimpse of their favourite pop star but the strategically positioned bouncers would soon encourage them to 'keep walking' if they loitered too close for comfort.

There were a few unremarkable characters peppered in and around Phoenix within the cordoned area. There was a beefed-up guy dressed in black whom he took to be Phoenix's personal bodyguard and two further people whom he recognised from media coverage: Phoenix's boyfriend Kaleb Rodriquez and her manager Neima Sage. As this was her club, Phoenix had been able to give strict instructions to the doormen not to allow any paparazzi in the establishment whatsoever.

Judd couldn't help but notice that Neima Sage looked somewhat agitated and she was keeping as close an eye on Phoenix as he was. Neima was pacing up and down, quite an achievement considering the height of her heels. Occasionally she spoke to people who approached her but she seemed preoccupied and certainly did not engage in any conversation which Judd could decipher by the swiftness in which they left her company. The manner in which she sipped at her champagne didn't suggest that she was enjoying the bubbling liquid either, instead, the placing of the expensive beverage to her full-lips seemed to be providing a coping technique for her tension, much as dragging on a cigarette may help those in a similarly anxious position.

Since becoming a PI, Judd had come to enjoy the pastime of people-watching and the displaying of body language on show tonight was particularly fascinating considering the stakes involved because what he hadn't expected to witness was the sloppiness of a personal bodyguard with the responsibility of protecting someone as famous as Phoenix. The bodyguard had incredibly turned his back on the crowd and therefore was not alive to any potential danger.

What happened next astonished Judd even further. Although the bodyguard's back was to Judd, Judd could make out that his hand had entered the pocket of his black bomber jacket and the shielding wasn't enough to block sight of him passing something into the palm of the hands of both Phoenix and Kaleb. The couple then moved out of the cordoned area into the nearby bathroom facilities which were not available for public use.

Judd had not been the only one to witness the transaction. Neima Sage had moved like lightning to pounce on the bodyguard, again quite an achievement considering the height of her shoes, and although Judd couldn't hear the words she was venting it was clear that a heated exchange was taking place.

"What did you give her this time you lowlife?"

"Chill, Neima. Do you need a little something yourself?"

"Was it heroin?"

The bodyguard didn't answer.

"Answer me you prick. Was it heroin?"

"Phoenix is old enough to make her own decisions."

"So, it was you bastard. You're hired to protect Phoenix and just like that parasitical boyfriend of hers you're party to destroying her."

"You shouldn't speak about my cousin that way, it's not nice. Besides Phoenix is happy with the arrangement."

"That's because you're turning her into an addict."

"She doesn't need my help for that. She makes her own choices."

"Choices that are heavily influenced by you and your scummy cousin."

"It's just simple supply and demand, Neima. I supply what Phoenix demands."

"I want you off the payroll."

"And who's going to protect your little girl then?"

"She's in more danger with you around. You're fired, now get the fuck out of here."

Judd didn't like what he saw next. After Neima had delivered her attempt at giving the bodyguard a dressing down he saw her grab her arm as she turned to walk away. "Phoenix employs me, not you. And while she's going steady with my cousin and I'm giving her what she needs I ain't going nowhere." Then the bodyguard grabbed Neima by the face, squeezing it hard which distorted her pretty features.

Neima felt scared.

The bodyguard was turning nastier by the Nano-second. "No wonder Phoenix uses drugs having a dragon like you suppressing her every five minutes. You know what, I reckon I could actually convince her to get rid of *you* instead of me. You see this hand I have around your weathered old mush? Well, I have Phoenix Easter right in the palm of it. And if you push me any further you may just find this hand around your throat one night while you lie frigid and alone in your bed."

Judd had seen enough. He identified that two bouncers were manning the steps into the cordoned area so he ran through the crowd and easily hurdled the roped barrier in order to get to the fracas. The bodyguard had no time to react as Judd smashed him in the temple causing him to loosen his grip on Neima and stumble away from her.

"Are you ok?" asked Judd. The wide-eyed Neima Sage nodded.

"You're going to regret doing that mister," said the

bodyguard regaining some composure.

"Really? It looks to me as if you're only capable of bullying women."

Infuriated, the bodyguard went for Judd but Judd blocked the punch before putting him on his arse again with a punch that split the bodyguard's lip.

By now the bouncers had sensed something was going down and they had got close enough to almost grab Judd when Neima raised her hand signalling for them to leave him alone.

She stood over the bleeding wreck on the floor. "Now you listen to me you piece of shit. You're fired. You are no longer Phoenix's bodyguard. If I have to I'll involve the police if you come anywhere near us again, and yes, I know what that would mean for Phoenix, but it's better than her occupying an early grave because of you."

Neima turned to the bouncers. "Get this piece of filth out of here boys, and feel free to achieve the objective in any way you see fit."

The bodyguard knew better than to try and resist the bouncers manhandling of him and before long he was ejected from the premises.

Neima turned to Judd. "Thank you, for helping me out there."

"I don't like seeing a lady in distress."

"What's your name?"

"Judd."

"Nice name, I'm Neima."

Judd smiled. "I know who you are."

"Allow me to buy you a drink Judd, it's the least I can do."

"The pleasure would be mine if you permit me to buy you one."

"Thank you, but I need to show my appreciation for rescuing me back there."

"There are many ways you can show me your appreciation... Oops, sorry that came out wrong." Judd hoped that the dim lighting of the club had camouflaged his blushes.

Neima smiled. Judd noticed that she had a lovely warm smile. "Don't apologise. You certainly know how to handle yourself, Judd. I have a proposition for you. Or maybe even two. Let me tell you all about it over that drink that one of us is going to buy."

CHAPTER 17
THE TAKING OF OPPORTUNITY

"Good morning, Judd. Or should I say Stud."

Judd shook himself awake and turned to face Neima who was supporting her head with the palm of her right hand as her arm created a forty-five-degree angle. Her gorgeous dark-brown hair straddled the arm and not for the first time Judd realised that her exotic and classy appearance reminded her a little of Gia Talia.

"Blimey, I slept like a log," said Judd rubbing his eyes.

"Well, I'm not surprised considering the amount of energy you used last night."

Judd smiled as he quickly reflected on the previous night's events. He couldn't help drawing on more comparisons. Like Gia, Neima also knew what she was doing in the sack.

However, Neima was definitely every inch a woman in her own right and unlike Gia, Judd could sense a vulnerability about the woman who lay before him. She simply seemed a really nice and genuine person.

"Last night was fantastic, Neima. It really was, but there's something you should know."

"Shhh…" Neima placed her finger on Judd's lips to silence him. "Don't worry, I'm guessing that a nice guy like you must have someone in his life. I'm cool with that, last night was just the coming together of two people who took advantage of an opportunity as it arose. We must ensure that no one gets hurt so we can be grown up about this."

"Well, there's not exactly someone in my life at the moment."

"Oh really! Well, you do surprise me, but no harm done then."

"I fucked things up with her, it's what I do, but I still love her and I'm not really ready for another relationship just yet, even though you're a great lady."

"Mmmm, similar circumstances to me it would seem. A woman has her needs Judd Stone and you were there for me last night, in more ways than one seeing off that jerk, Ziggy. But like you, I love someone else and I'm not looking for a relationship with you or anyone else for that matter. No offence."

"None taken. Ziggy? That's the name of the bodyguard?"

"Ex-bodyguard. Yeah, Ziggy is his name not that there's much stardust about him. It seemed only proper that I should thank you for coming to my rescue like that."

"Well, you certainly thanked me incredibly well, Neima. I'm a little worn out if truth be told."

Neima smiled. "So, who is she?"

"Who?"

"This crazy girl who you love but is too dumb to be by your side."

"Her name is Brooke. She's not dumb, Neima. She has every right to hate me. I cheated on her and she found out."

"Ahh, and she couldn't forgive you?"

"No, it's complicated. What about you? Who's the guy you love? And by the way, he's a jerk not to want to be with you."

"I haven't told this person that I love them."

"Why not?"

"It's complicated."

"Well, it looks like neither of us did anything wrong last night then?"

"You bet we didn't, and I see no reason why we can't do it again. We both like to have fun and we both know where we stand."

"Well, that sounds a reasonable proposal, Miss Sage."

"And what about my other proposal? Have you had enough time to think about it?"

"I'm not sure. I already have a job."

"And Phoenix needs a bodyguard and I need someone I can trust. The way you handled Ziggy I can see that you'd be an ideal recruitment. You clearly have experience of dealing with confrontational situations in a very efficient way."

"You could say that."

"I don't mean to be churlish, but I'm sure you can imagine how well paid a bodyguard to a famous pop star would be compared to the more average occupation."

"It had crossed my mind."

It had also crossed Judd's mind that becoming Phoenix's bodyguard would place him in the most perfect position possible to protect her from entering the 27 club, a concept he chose not to currently share with the singer's manager. He marvelled at how he had managed to inadvertently find himself in this position to honour the agreement he had made with Ben Francis and his niece Xanthe, let alone his own increasing personal desire to protect Phoenix from harm.

"Well, I'll need to sort a few things out with my investigative work, but in reality, how can I turn down a job like this. I accept your kind proposal, Neima. Of course, I'll be Phoenix Easter's bodyguard."

"Well, in that case, Mr. Stone, I will have to show you

my appreciation once again."

"It's the only reason I took the job," joked Judd, before he was silenced as Neima's tongue entered his mouth.

.

CHAPTER 18
THE BODYGUARD

"So, you're my new bodyguard?" asked Phoenix casting a mischievous smile across her pretty face which revealed her trademark golden-capped maxillary canine tooth. Being this close to the rock star, Judd could fully appreciate Phoenix's stunning features. No-one on earth looked like Phoenix, it was if she had been purposefully created to be one of a kind. However, in spite of her natural beauty, being this close enabled Judd to also notice the telling signs of drug and alcohol abuse. Phoenix was wearing very little make-up. Her eyes were red, her lips were dry and her hair was a little unkempt. Judd could tell that maintaining her appearance was not currently the priority for Miss. Phoenix Easter.

"Yes, I am. Judd's the name."

"Pleased to meet you, Judd."

They exchanged a handshake, and now that Judd had actually touched the superstar before him his surreal situation escalated even further.

"And I'm Ocran le Boeuf, I represent Phoenix at her Record Company."

Judd had been so taken with Phoenix that he had hardly noticed that she was being accompanied by the tall man in the expensive suit and shoes. He was as well-spoken as Warwick Stansfield had been and he was one of those people who instantly annoyed Judd by delivering a much stronger than was necessary handshake. It was as if even in that first moment he was trying to assert a superior level of authority.

Judd quickly returned his attention to Phoenix. "I need you to know, Phoenix, that I won't be supplying you with any drugs like the last joker who had been hired to protect you."

Phoenix delivered another winning smile. "If I want drugs I'll get drugs. So, can Kaleb. Ziggy was just a convenience on that score. He wasn't just a joker he was a complete dick. I know that. I only hired him as a favour to Kaleb, because he was Kaleb's cousin."

"There's no need to worry, Judd. Phoenix has the drugs under control. Anyway, it's good for the image and record sales."

Judd shot Ocran a menacing look.

"I'm joking of course," said the man from the record company placing his hands in the air in an exaggerated open gesture.

This guy was irritating Judd by the second, but Phoenix balanced the situation by continuing to enchant her new employee.

"Take no notice of Ocran, Judd. He has a very select sense of humour. Besides, I have a bodyguard to protect me, now don't I?" Phoenix's eyes were flirty as she took out a cigarette and lit it with a brilliant-white coloured lighter before blowing the smoke seductively towards Judd. "I'm glad I have a big strong man like you around, Judd. And if Neima thinks you're the right man for the job then you're the man. I trust Neima, she takes good care of me."

"She cares a lot about you?"

"She worries too much."

"She may have good reason."

Phoenix blew out smoke once again, this time it escaped from the corner of her mouth. "Don't go all Kevin Costner on me, Judd."

"Huh?"

"You know - the film - *The Bodyguard*. Costner is hired to protect Whitney's character and he gets a little paranoid around her. That's not gonna happen to you is it?"

Judd smiled. "Ahh, ok I'm with you. However, if I recall correctly, Costner's character was ultimately proved to be very wise to have remained so vigilant."

"Then perhaps I'm lucky to have you, Judd."

Phoenix stood on her tiptoes and kissed Judd on the cheek before they said their temporary goodbyes.

Judd didn't wash his face for a week.

.

CHAPTER 19
THE UNLIKELY ANGEL

Juggling two jobs was proving to be very difficult for Judd. Never the naturally tidiest of people and being somewhat of a technophobe born out of his lack of patience, Judd was one of those people whose ways of working could never fully rely on the advancing means of digital and electronic devices. Coupled with the extra investment of hours that he was spending in his quest to protect Phoenix the paperwork connected with his other private investigations was building up to form a small range of mountains. He had lost track of his invoices and he was no longer clear as to who owed him what or who had settled their payments for his services. Judd was also all over the place concerning his self-assessment tax return.

Now Judd had opened his mind to many things since he learned of his favourite couple's abilities to perform extraordinary acts. His best friend William Chamberlain was telekinetic and William's fiancée, Crystal Stance, was able to connect with the dead. So, when a young Asian girl appeared at his Rotunda home-come-workplace he seriously wondered if he had been sent an angel once the conversation unfolded.

"Hello, Judd. You look like you could need some help."

"I wouldn't deny that. It's all this damn paperwork."

"You look like shit. Haven't you been sleeping very well?"

Judd was a little taken aback at the young girl's directness, however, he couldn't argue with her assessment of him. "Err, not great I guess."

The young girl's eyes decidedly scanned Judd's residence, disapproval written all across her face.

"Judd, you live like a pig. How long have you been piling up those takeaway cartons over there?"

"Err, a while I guess. Look, who exactly are you?"

"I believe Ganesh must have had a part to play in sending me to you and to assist with clearing your obstacles in life, and boy there are many obstacles from where I'm standing."

"Ganesh?"

"Never mind, you'll be more familiar with my sister. She said that you could do with some help but she never told me that you were this much of a slob."

"I've been busy," Judd was surprised at how he found himself justifying his living conditions to a total stranger. Although slight in build, the young girl before him was formidable in character. "Does your sister know me?"

"I'm Yasmin, my sister is Sab."

"Ahh, the penny drops. You're Sab's younger sister. She often speaks about you, she says you can be a bit of a handful, although I can't think why."

Yasmin was instantly irritated. "Is that what she said about me? She can be so annoying. She's on the other side of the Atlantic and she still manages to be a controlling freak."

"Perhaps you can explain why you are here, Yasmin?"

"Ever since I dropped out of Uni, my golden-titted sister has been on at me to get a job. She told me she had this friend who had just started up as a Private Investigator and would undoubtedly need some administrative help. It looks like she knows you only too well, Judd."

Judd smiled. He had always liked Sab. "Mmmm, a bit of her has always leaned towards being a control freak and perhaps a bit of her always will be, but clearly her intentions are good. Well, it certainly looks like I could need the help, doesn't it? There's no point in my denying it."

"I won't take less than a tenner an hour."

"A tenner? How old are you?"

"Nineteen."

"That's not minimum wage."

"Who said anything about minimum wage. Just look at the amount of shit that I've got to get through. I can demand more if you like?"

Judd instantly buckled. "Ok, ok you're hired. Ten quid an hour and not a penny more."

"Great, I'll start straight away."

"Good…I think…you do that. Look, I'm very busy at the moment Yasmin, I'll tell you about it sometime but right now it would blow your mind if you knew what else I was up to."

"Don't worry, I know all about you Judd. For instance, I know that you're a bodyguard for Phoenix Easter."

"Oh, so Sab told you that?"

"Yep. It's probably the only reason I agreed to help you. I'm a huge Phoenix fan."

"Fair enough, but I'm not sure how much I can involve you in that side of my work."

"That's a shame, I'm sure I could help. You believe that you need to protect Miss Easter from entering the 27 club, don't you?

Judd was amazed that Yasmin knew this as he hadn't discussed the 27 club with her sister. "How do you know that?"

"Come on, it doesn't take a genius to work out. She's

approaching 27 and she fits the profile perfectly, but I can also tell you a whole lot more from a very different angle."

"Go on."

"You know me and Sab are Hindu right?"

"I do."

"Well the origins of our religion date back as long ago as 1500 Before Common Era – BCE. Or you're probably more familiar with the terminology BC – Before Christ. Whichever floats your boat, it doesn't really matter. This period of time in relation to what I'm about to tell you was known as the Vedic Period."

"The Vedic Period? Ok, I'm not familiar with it as far as I know but it sounds intriguing."

"The most sacred books of India are known as the Vedas which originate from the Vedic Period. The Vedas are the literary record of the original Hindu teachings and hold unrivalled spiritual knowledge and wisdom. The Vedas teaches us the prominence of women as being the embodiment of spiritual and intellectual fulfilment. Goddesses and not just Gods were taken seriously at this time and 27 women seers derived from the literary teachings who were presented through a series of Myriad Hymns."

"27. There's that number again. Forgive my ignorance but what is a seer?"

"As its sounds a see-er, someone who can see things others can't. So, in other words, a Prophet. Someone who possesses the profound wisdom, knowledge and spiritual intellect to provide insight into future events."

"The more dedicated fans of Phoenix Easter have often referred to her as being a prophet. She's a talented woman alright but I've always felt that that section of her fans were getting carried away with that one."

"Think about it, Judd. Phoenix's lyrics often provide knowledge, wisdom and spiritual insight way beyond her 26 years. Only a fool would deny her unique ability as a lyricist and a musician."

"Ok, but you're not suggesting that she's a goddess, surely?"

"Of course not, but she is a dominant woman of this period that we currently stand in. She is and should be listened to. Both Vedic teachings and history tells us, no let me rephrase that, screams out at us, that women with special talent should not be underestimated because they provide profound spiritual and societal importance. Phoenix is respected as an artist but also as a representative voice for many. She has the foresight to provide thought-provoking lyrics regarding the world we live in today and more importantly what's coming down the line. Her lyrics have transcended environmental, political and social attitudes but history also tells us that visionaries like Phoenix often give way for their cause."

"Ain't that the truth."

"And what better way is there for Phoenix to be sacrificed for her own credible cause or someone else's warped cause by entering the 27 Club?"

Judd stroked the stubble on his chin, the growth of facial hair representing another indication of the compromising of his time. "I can't deny that's interesting stuff Yasmin and I certainly need to stay on my toes in order to protect Phoenix it would seem. You've given me plenty food for thought there, I have a very open mind with most things. It seems there are arrows of fate being lined up for her all over the place. But coming back down to earth it is the administrative side of my work where I need your help. You said so yourself."

"I know. Besides, if I help you any more with Phoenix I'll want double my salary thank you very much. I just wanted to highlight to you just how an acute possibility it is that Phoenix is under threat to enter the 27 Club."

"Thank you. You achieved your aim very well. You've made me realise that I need to focus even harder on protecting Phoenix, which makes it clear that I need to augment my PI enterprise if that's not to suffer as a consequence."

"And how are you going to do that?"

"I have an idea."

CHAPTER 20
THE ARRANGEMENT

"Keep away from me, Stone. One step nearer and I'll phone the police." Ted had cowered behind his desk in order to form a barrier of protection.

"Relax, Ted. I come in peace."

"Relax? The last time we met you put me in the hospital and you expect me to relax around you?"

"Ted, please take it easy. I'm not here to hurt you. In fact, I apologise unreservedly for attacking you. I have no excuse but I was upset because you were the instrument used by Brooke which resulted in me losing her and I took everything out on you. I now know that I only have myself to blame for losing her. You were just doing your job and you did it well. I've served my time, Ted, and deservingly so. I've been punished for what I did to you and being without Brooke means that I continue to be punished every single day. But that's my fault and my fault alone. I am truly sorry."

Ted was curious but managed to relax slightly. "So, what do you want?"

"I have a proposition for you."

"Blackmail?"

"No, nothing like that. Ted, you really do need to chill. Stop being on duty just for a minute. Please. Now, tell me. How's business?"

"Patchy at best."

"So, you would benefit from increasing your workload, perhaps?"

"Yes, I guess so."

"Then I may be able to help you, and then hopefully we can put all of this behind us. Who knows we may even become friends."

Ted Armstrong looked puzzled. He had concluded that Judd Stone was crazy long ago but now he was demonstrating a new kind of crazy. He was being friendly.

"What if I were to tell you that you inspired me, Ted?"

"Inspired you? Me? But how?"

"I lost my job as DCI after giving you the once over, Ted. I needed to find alternative means to make a living so guess what? I decided to become a private investigator, just like you."

"You did, huh?"

"Yep, and now something's come up that's going to keep me very busy for a while. I could really do with temporarily placing my caseload in the hands of someone I can trust. And that someone is you, Ted."

"Me, but why?"

"You are obviously a good PI, Ted. I know that better than anybody don't I?"

"So, what's the catch?"

"There's no catch, I just need someone to take on my PI work for a while. If I don't my business is going to go under, no question. And I guess that I still feel I owe you even after serving at Her Majesty's Pleasure, or something like that."

"I don't know, Stone. It could be dangerous getting into bed with you. If I do something you don't like you're likely to give me another kicking."

"I won't interfere, mate. I'm going to be far too busy doing other things, believe me. I have a new secretary too who can help run things in the background, so she'll help alleviate any administrative pressure. You'll have no trouble from her, she's a very straightforward kind of a girl."

Ted was still unconvinced but he knew he needed more work and the bills were beginning to stack up. He amazed himself with the directness of his next sentence, but perhaps it showed how Judd's warm persona was beginning to thaw the previous hostility between the two men. "If I agree, I keep 80% of the intake."

"I was thinking closer to 100%, Ted."

Ted's eyes widened. "That seems very generous of you, Judd. Are you sure there is no catch?"

"I'm being paid very handsomely for this other line of work that I'm involved in. I just need you to keep my business ticking over until I'm back, and I don't know how long that is going to be so it will be a nice little earner for you. I've got work coming out of my ears. I just need to ensure Yasmin's wages are covered and the rest of the income is yours."

"Yasmin is the straightforward secretary?"

"Yep. She's a diamond. You'll be glad you have her. So what d'ya say?" Judd held out his hand.

"This doesn't necessarily mean that I forgive you, Judd."

"Purely business my friend. Come on you're smarter than to look a gift horse in the mouth. I'm simply supplementing your workload and therefore your financial intake, whilst I'm safe in the knowledge that I have the best caretaker I could possibly hope for to take care of my PI business. What d'ya say?" Judd continued to hold out his hand to the Private Investigator.

For the first time, Ted Armstrong smiled. "Ok, it's a deal."

The two men shook hands.

CHAPTER 21
THE PRESS CONFERENCE

Phoenix Easter finally arrived at the press conference almost two hours later than scheduled. True to form she had snorted a small amount of cocaine before vacating her hotel room but to Neima's relief, her prodigy was to be fully coherent and in top charismatic form.

Phoenix had chosen Birmingham's five-star Radisson Blu Hotel for the press conference, it was important to her to announce her intentions in the bosom of her home city, and as she had stayed there the night before there really had been no excuse for her late entrance. Phoenix had left Kaleb flat out in the luxury bed whilst she took centre stage, or rather centre table, whilst Neima sat to her left and Judd found himself in the latest surreal position of sitting to Phoenix's right.

The press and media were willing to forgive Phoenix for keeping them waiting, they knew that this press conference had been called for something special and they were grateful that they were the ones who had been chosen to report on an undoubted piece of musical history.

For all of her off-stage problems, musically, Phoenix was at the top of her game and stood head and shoulders above her contemporary peers who were totally unable to rival her unique talent.

The atmosphere amongst the salivating journalists was almost tangible. It was true that due to her drunken and naturally wild ways of living, Phoenix constantly provided them with an abundance of juicy material that sold tabloid newspapers by the lorry load, but equally the media recognised just what a raw and unprecedented talent Phoenix truly was so they were always overjoyed to soak up anything that Phoenix had to offer in a professional capacity.

The rumour had been that Phoenix was going to announce a forthcoming live tour, something the world was eager to see, but the word had been that this tour would be unlike anything ever witnessed before. Exactly why this tour would be different from any other was anybody's guess, but the journalists were eagerly dying to know.

Although the occupants of the room were eager to hang on Phoenix's every word, it was Neima who actually opened proceedings. "Ladies and Gentlemen, thank you for taking the time to attend this very exciting press conference. In a moment I'll hand you over to Phoenix who will reveal the details of why we have asked you to join us today. Following Phoenix's announcement, we will allow a short session for questions, so please can I ask you to refrain from speaking until that time is clearly evident. Thank you for your cooperation. Now with no more further ado, Ladies and Gentlemen, I give you Phoenix."

The audience waited with baited breath as Phoenix took a long swig of her glass of water, composing herself for what she was about to reveal and heightening the anticipation. Finally, she spoke.

"Ladies and Gentlemen of the Press, thank you for sharing this moment with me today. What I want to reveal to you is a little ambitious, a little unprecedented but is something that I am going to incredibly enjoy. Starting in just a few weeks from now I am going to embark on a world tour, but it will be a world tour like no other. It will take in only a small number of concerts, but the venues have been very carefully selected to achieve an unrivalled musical and theatrical experience as you will soon come to understand. These concerts will become part of musical history, of that I am one-hundred percent confident. So, would you like to know more?"

Phoenix couldn't help but tease the gathering and her trademark gold tooth sparkled as her face beamed the widest smile when the audience responded with a resounding, "Yes, yes, yes."

She took a drink of water once more in order to increase the tension. Finally, she spoke again. "Ok, ok. I'll tell you."

The members of the press were on the edge of their seats.

Judd scanned the faces in the room, partly to exercise the vigilant duty of being a bodyguard who was looking out for his client, but he was also in awe of Phoenix and her ability to control these unscrupulous people who sat before her. He was impressed.

"I am going to perform my concerts at the most historical sites in history. In 1985 Wham! became the first western band to play in China. This was truly a historic moment and I lay down my gratitude to George Michael and Andrew Ridgeley for paving the way for artists like me. However, I am to go one better than the boys from Bushey by performing a concert at the Great Wall of China itself. I will also be performing amongst the Pyramids of Egypt, at the base of the Eiffel Tower in Paris and beneath the backdrop of the Christ the Redeemer statue in Rio De Janeiro, Brazil. Other confirmed locations include the Berlin Wall Memorial, New York's Central Park, Mount Rushmore with the four presidents cheering me on and personally I can't wait to perform at my own personal favourite of the spectacular locations of the tour: The Grand Canyon in Arizona. I'm afraid the latter may have me so excited that I'm likely to pee my pants live on stage so there's a world exclusive you'll all want a piece of... Or maybe not."

The audience of the press all laughed along with Phoenix.

"Being serious for a moment, I want you all to know that I will also be using these iconic locations as a platform to raise awareness of the humanitarian, environmental and animal equality matters which I hold close to my heart.

"In addition to the fascinating venues I have already mentioned, Neima is leading negotiations for further performances at Chichen Itza in Mexico, the grounds of the Taj Mahal and either Vatican Square or the Coliseum in Rome, but as I'm sure you can appreciate there are some obvious hurdles to get over in securing some of these aspirational venues, not least we wish to fully respect any spiritual or religious significance that these locations hold. Now, are there any questions?"

Neima stepped in to facilitate the excitement in the room. She allowed the first question to derive from a lesser-known journalist from an Independent Birmingham Radio station, much to the annoyance of the bigger fish in the room.

"Yes, Sandy. Please go ahead."

Sandy couldn't believe her luck. "The tour sounds absolutely amazing, Phoenix, and some of the venues you mention will undoubtedly make musical history when a concert is held there. I couldn't help noticing however that there was no mention of any British venues. Won't your home-grown fans be a little bemused if you don't play any concerts here at home?"

Phoenix didn't hesitate in responding. "I'm very glad you mentioned that, Sandy. Thank you. As part of the tour, I will, of course, play Wembley stadium, an arena that needs no introduction for iconic status. For the purposes of the press conference, I was initially just homing in on the more unconventional venues. The full programme of concerts will be published in due course on my website. Additionally, either side of Wembley, I will play Hyde Park and a venue that I believe I can once again reveal as being a first for hosting a rock concert: The Tower of London. And don't worry, Sandy, I won't be turning my back on my home city either. I'll be playing Sutton Park, not quite a world first but certainly an unusual choice and I'm kicking the tour off with a free gig on the rooftop of our very own iconic Rotunda building."

Judd nearly fell off his chair. He had no idea that Phoenix was planning a concert on top of his home!

Neima allowed a more well-known journalist from the BBC to ask the next question. "The tour sounds truly wonderful, Phoenix. What on earth gave you such a novel idea to perform at such a collection of ambitious and historic venues?"

"To be honest with you Sir Paul McCartney toyed with the idea for The Beatles to play these types of concerts back in the late sixties, but the idea never came to fruition due to the well-documented differences the band were having at that time and the lack of appetite to play live, instead preferring to concentrate on the amazing music that we all know transpired in the studios of Abbey Road. Now, how often do any of us get a chance to do something that The Beatles had never even achieved, so once I thought about it seriously it was a no-brainer really. That's one of the reasons why I'm doing the rooftop gig at The Rotunda, it's kind of my tribute to the rooftop gig they performed at 3 Saville Row in 1969 and for giving me the idea of what my world tour needed to be."

"Are there any more traditional venues on the tour, similar to Wembley Stadium?" continued the BBC journalist.

"Well, the tour is to be called 'The Wonderful World

Tour.' I want everyone to share in the celebration of our wonderful planet while we still can, but the tour will include the more regular venues which remain wonderful in their own right such as Sydney Opera House, the Olympic Stadium in Athens, AC Milan's San Siro stadium, Barcelona's Nou Camp and another British venue will be utilised as I'll be performing in the grounds of Derbyshire's Chatsworth House."

The exciting questions and dialogue flowed much more than they ebbed but Judd's attention drifted away from the words in the room when he suddenly spotted someone curiously using the exit door at the rear of the premises.

Who would want to leave such a fascinating press conference? He thought.

Judd had been unable to catch sight of the person's face only noticing the figure on its departure, but what was even more curious and what had grabbed his attention just like an icy grip on his throat by the abominable snowman, was the fact that this man was carrying a black umbrella.

CHAPTER 22
A FRIEND IN NEED

Knowing only too well the significance of the man with the umbrella, Judd moved swiftly and without apology, much to the bemusement of Phoenix, Neima and the gathering of press personnel. Nevertheless, the captivating press conference continued minus the presence of Phoenix's bodyguard.

By the time Judd had reached the elevator the doors were already closing shut, but there was just enough time for Judd to spot the handle of an umbrella and the fading bowed head of its owner. Frustratingly, Judd still didn't know what this guy actually looked like in the face.

"Shit!" was all he could verbally offer himself as he furiously banged at the elevator buttons whilst helplessly watching the numbers of each floor take their turn to light up and then fade as the elevator descended.

Judd frantically looked around and noticed the door to the fire escape. Realising this was his only option, he kicked open the door, then continued with purposeful momentum as he ran down the umpteen flights of stairs in a bid to reach the ground floor and catch hold of the Umbrella Man in order to ask him some very searching questions.

A couple of minutes or so later a panting Judd Stone screwed his face up in frustration at the realisation that the Umbrella Man had already evaded him. Judd could plainly see the vacant elevator as an elderly woman and what Judd took to be her granddaughter step into the now empty vessel.

Judd gathered enough breath to run across the hotel reception foyer and out onto the street, looking first to his left down Smallbrook Queensway, then a few steps forward enabled him to look along part of Bristol Street and then slightly shift his gaze beyond the twelve-metre-high Chinese Pagoda into the beginnings of Bath Row. Then he looked right towards the New Alexandra Theatre and the Mailbox, searching all angles of Suffolk Street Queensway, but amongst the sea of shoppers, diners and congested traffic it was impossible to pick out the Umbrella Man.

In desperation, Judd rushed back into the hotel demanding information. First, he tried the concierge who looked at him as if he was mad when he shouted: "Did you see a man leave here carrying an umbrella?"

Realising the concierge had clearly not seen anything of the kind, Judd turned his attention to a hotel receptionist. "I'm sorry sir, I didn't notice anyone of that description. Why did he have an umbrella, it's very hot in Birmingham today?"

"Good question," answered Judd. "Are you sure you never saw him?"

"Quite sure."

"Damn."

Judd moved away from the bewildered receptionist, uncharacteristically failing to absorb her seductive accent and pretty features such was the impact of the situation. Standing alone, helpless in the hotel foyer it was one of those occasions where he wished he was still working side by side with his old friend and pillar of stability, William Chamberlain. As a duo in Birmingham and District CID, they were unrivalled as crime fighters. Judd was still good friends with William, but since their lives had naturally drifted apart from once being virtually in one another's pockets, Judd at times found himself feeling lost and longing for his friend's words of wisdom.

The moment with Umbrella Man had unfortunately gone, so he pulled out his mobile phone with the intent to give his best friend a call. There was no point in discussing what had just happened, but the presence of the Umbrella Man, assuming he really was *the* Umbrella Man, had shaken Judd as he fully recognised what his presence could mean. How was he expected to protect Phoenix from such an enigma? This Umbrella Man seemed likely to be some kind of supernatural entity he concluded, and Judd's mind was more than open to such things. Judd had already found the mysterious being's presence in the photos of all of those prematurely deceased people of fame unsettling, but now on top of that, it did seem as though this Umbrella Man had simply vanished into thin air!

Judd needed to hear his friends voice. That'd be enough, for now, just a chat with his old buddy to bring him back to sanity.

As it happened a friendly voice was forthcoming to help lift Judd's mood. But it wasn't to be William. As Judd went to punch in the zero to begin the call to his dearest friend, he was prevented from doing so as his phone rang into life. Judd smiled as he saw the photo image and name of another very dear pal appear on the screen of the phone.

"Sab, how the hell are you?"

"I'm good thanks, Judd. How about you? How's things with my old buddy, the bodyguard to the stars?"

"Oh, I'm ok." He quickly realised, despite the appearance of the Umbrella Man, as things stood Phoenix was perfectly safe and actually in her element while she sat upstairs with the press drooling in the palm of her hand. "I'm really good, thanks Sab. But hey, I may be the bodyguard of *a* star but you're the one living the dream, you must be seeing the rich and famous every single day."

"And arresting some of 'em."

"Really? Wow! So, how is life in LAPD?"

"It's pretty cool."

"Why are you talking in an American accent, you phoney?"

"Fuck you."

"Fuck you? How very American. Have you forgotten your roots Miss. Mistry?"

"Alroight, jog on yow prick." Sab had put on an exaggerated Brummie accent to enhance the friendly banter.

"Now that's more like it, girl."

"How's my sister?"

"Scary."

"Ha, ha. I knew she'd be a good influence on you. With me across the pond and William not around as much I knew Yasmin would keep a much-needed eye on you."

"Keep an eye on me? She's like a wicked step-mother even though she's much younger than me!"

"That sounds like my little sis. She can be a little direct, but her heart's in the right place."

"She's a bit of a control freak if I'm being honest, must run in the family hey?"

"Cheeky!"

"You know, if it wasn't for the age gap I'd say she's got this 'love-hate' thing going on with me."

"Nah mate, you're definitely not her type, believe me."

"And how can you say that with such certainty?"

"Because she's gay."

"Oh, right. Ok. Wow, I couldn't tell, I mean not that I should have been able to necessarily."

"Believe it or not, not all women are placed on this Earth to fall at your feet, Judd."

"So, it seems. Well, she's efficient in her work I'll give her that. She's doing a great job, she's got my business very organised."

"Like I say, she'll look after you."

"Anyway, it seems I'm coming over the pond too."

"Really?"

"Really."

"Oh, Judd it would be so great to see you."

"Yeah, Phoenix has just announced a special kind of world tour which is gonna take in the Grand Canyon, so although it's not exactly down the road from where you are I'll sort you out a ticket."

"Wow, that is certainly a different type of concert venue. Well let me know when you're over and I'll sort out my shifts. I ain't gonna miss a concert like that for the world."

"You bet. I may even drag the old boy over too, I'm sure he could do with a holiday. It'll be like the three musketeers back together again"

"More like a dysfunctional Bananarama. Seriously, it'll be great to hook up again. And Crystal would love it over here, especially Vegas – that'll be right up her street."

"Yeah, she could probably predict the turn of the cards or the throw of the dice. She'd walk away a millionaire."

"Huh?"

"Oh, never mind. Do you think William will be fit enough to travel, you know, because of his MS?"

"Judd, you know the steel of the man, let alone his stubbornness. Wild horses won't be able to stop him."

"You're right. He can be a determined dude all right."

"Dude? And you call me an American phoney. At least I'm living here."

"Sab, it's going to be a reunion to remember."

Judd was yet to know just how memorable it was going to be.

CHAPTER 23
THE HOUNDS OF HELL

"The vultures are circling Judd, we need to do something," said a desperate Neima Sage as she spotted the press accumulating around the nightspots of the Arcadian - a popular area of Birmingham's bar and club scene. With two of the city's theatres situated in the area, the location could loosely be described as Birmingham's smaller version of London's West End.

Phoenix Easter was excessively drunk and had become involved in hurling the most torrid and offensive abuse at anyone who she happened to come into contact with, much to the amusement of her boyfriend Kaleb Rodriguez.

The troubled superstar had been on the mightiest pub crawl that spanned the breadth of Birmingham's city centre and it was only when she had telephoned Neima with a spat of slurred expletives that Neima had fully realised just what an acute intoxicated state the girl that she cared so much for was in. Although Phoenix's words were spiteful, Neima knew better than to take them to heart. It wasn't the first time Phoenix had become aggressive whilst drunk and once she became sober she would never recollect any memory of her outlandish behaviour.

Neima was also fully aware of Kaleb's hatred towards her and as he would bad-mouth her at any given opportunity Neima knew that this could only serve to stir-up Phoenix once she hit the bottle.

Judd and Neima had found Phoenix crumpled in a heap at the side of the Birmingham Hippodrome theatre, somehow managing to stagger there after frequenting every single bar in the vicinity of Birmingham's Gay Village. Kaleb was dancing around like a laughing hyena drawing even more unwanted attention to the situation. His state suggested that he'd taken something much stronger than just alcohol.

Judd attempted to raise Phoenix to her feet but the singer was a dead weight and her legs were buckling like jelly. "Leave me alone, you tosser. I want another fucking drink."

"You heard her Stone, leave her alone," spat Kaleb. "Why don't you fuck off out of here and stop interfering with our night out."

"She's had enough, Kaleb. She needs to go home."

"I'll say when she needs to go home, now you take your fucking hands off my girlfriend."

Neima interjected. "You won't be happy until she's dead, will you Kaleb."

"Kaleb just laughed. "Oh, don't be so melodramatic you frigid piece of stuck-up shit. You can fuck off as well."

"Quite the charmer aren't you, Rodriguez?" said Judd.

"I thought I told you to take your fucking hands off my girlfriend."

"I'm trying to help her you prick, which is more than you've ever done."

"I'm warning you. Leave her alone, now."

As it happened Judd was having very little success with getting Phoenix to her feet so he left her be for a moment before taking a couple of steps closer to Kaleb. "Trust me, you don't want to do this Kaleb."

"Oh yes I do," and with those words, Kaleb foolishly took a swing at Judd which he was easily able to dodge by ducking the punch and following up with a much more meaningful punch of his own to Kaleb's stomach. The lowlife instantly crumpled to his knees and inadvertently began to vomit the night's contents from his stomach. A swift kick to the underside of his chin put Kaleb to sleep and out of harm's way.

"Judd, you've killed him!" screamed a startled Neima. Although no fan of Kaleb she was concerned about the obvious repercussions if Judd had indeed killed Phoenix's toxic boyfriend.

"Nah, he'll be alright. Come on, help me get Phoenix to her feet."

Judd and Neima took an arm each and as Phoenix flopped under their support she almost looked like a crucified messiah with her arms stretched out around their shoulders.

By now a rush of photographers had reached the scene with a section taking photographs of the unconscious Kaleb Rodriguez but the majority taking advantage of the prize which they all sought, a picture of a pissed-up Phoenix Easter. Phoenix really was the gift that just kept giving when it came to selling papers.

The clicks and whooshes of the cameras seemed to register something within Phoenix and she amazingly found some newborn energy. She managed to break free from Judd and Neima and in a flash she had leapt at one photographer scratching at his face and screaming expletives at him as his camera dropped to the floor.

Neima shouted at the crowd of parasites. "Is it any wonder she gets in this state? She can never have a private life because of you lot. You lot hounding her day in and day out applies an enormous amount of pressure on her. She drinks to escape you strangling her."

"Come off it, Neima," said one photographer. "She

doesn't need our help to go on the piss. Would you say she's taken any narcotics tonight as well?"

"Like I'd give any of you parasites a statement of any sort."

Judd, sensing the need to protect his superstar client in more ways than one, approached Phoenix from behind who was still assaulting the photographer and lifted her by the waist before placing her next to Neima. "Calm down, Phoenix. This is what they want."

"I'll fucking kill them all," she initially screamed.

"No, Phoenix, don't give them what they want."

Somehow it seemed Judd's words had suddenly managed to get through to the vulnerable superstar and Phoenix's unpredictive mood shifted again as she turned to Neima, buried her head into her friend's chest and began to sob uncontrollably.

Judd turned on a sixpence and stamped on the camera that had fallen to the floor rendering it useless. He then stood over the bleeding photographer who had managed to get to his knees. "Now listen to me and listen good. If you're thinking of pressing any charges against Phoenix I'll hunt you down and break every fucking finger and thumb on your dirty little hands so you'll never be able to wipe your arse again let alone take a fucking photograph. Do we understand one another you parasitic piece of filth?"

The photograph nodded in pathetic affirmation.

Judd then encouraged the rest of the paparazzi to move along in his own inimitable style.

Of course, at first, they disobeyed him and continued to click away like a pack of demented wolves taking photos of Phoenix as she wailed in a distressed state. However, when one unwise photographer had the audacity to place a hand on Judd's being the situation was soon brought to a halt. "Move aside fella, you're in the way of a good shot here," said the insolent photographer, but seconds later Judd had silenced him courtesy of a head-butt. After slapping a couple more of the disrespectful paparazzi, the entourage concluded that it was wise to retreat from the situation…and fast.

Just then as the coast began to finally clear, Neima's phone began to ring. "Hello…Sorry Ocran, this is not a good time right now. I am sorry. I'll call you back but it'll be much later I'm afraid." Neima killed the call as quickly as she had answered it.

"What did he want?" enquired Judd. There was something about that guy Judd didn't like but he couldn't quite put his finger on why. Perhaps he was just being over-protective and his valid distrust of Kaleb was enough to cloud his opinion of all the male figures in Phoenix's life.

"I don't know, I've had to cut him off for obvious reasons. I feel a bit bad, he's such a nice guy."

"Well you were right to cut the call, we have far more pressing matters to take care of and we need to sort Phoenix out. Come on we don't have time to worry about Ocran just now. I'm sure he'll cope."

As Judd and Neima helped Phoenix to her feet and into the nearby parked car, she had continued to shift quite markedly from an aggressive state to one of a teary depressive. She attempted to light a cigarette with her white lighter but couldn't coordinate her hands and quickly gave up. She uttered a single sentence before falling to sleep on the back seat. "I hate my fucking life."

CHAPTER 24
THE CONCERT ON THE ROOFTOP OF THE ROTUNDA

Phoenix Easter played the opening guitar chord of her monster hit "The Demons Within" and smiled as it rang out across the blue suburban sky of Birmingham. "A Hard Day's Night" by The Beatles had perhaps been the only other track so heavily defined by its opening chord, therefore Phoenix's choice of opener proved a fitting one considering hers was now the most famous rooftop concert since the one that took place on top of 3 Savile Row, London on 30 January 1969.

The familiar infectious drumbeat of the track kicked in for an extended period compared to the recorded track, dramatically prolonged to build the tension of this much-anticipated concert. The crowds that swarmed the city centre streets could hardly believe the time had now come for the performance and they were finally rewarded and freed from their torment once Phoenix's distinctive voice began to sing out the lyrics to her self-penned song.

Judd could hardly believe the envious position he found himself to be in. Here he was standing on the rooftop of his own home just yards from the greatest singer-songwriter of her generation as she made history and provided a faultless performance. Being this close to Phoenix he could fully appreciate the unique talent and stage presence that she naturally and effortlessly exhibited. Once on stage Phoenix was an entirely different person from the drunken and troubled girl she seemed to be in day to day life. Judd marvelled at how healthy and happy she looked, performing it seemed was what she had been created for.

Judd had managed to secure the same view on the rooftop for Ben's niece Xanthe, Sadie and Yasmin and the small collective watched on mesmerised at Phoenix's jaw-dropping performance. Neima was also standing with them.

Kaleb hadn't bothered to turn up to witness his girlfriend make history. He was no doubt too busy lying in a pool of his own vomit or coming down from an illegal high of some description. His lack of presence didn't bother Judd or Neima, they often discussed the negative impact he had on Phoenix, but the principle of him not being bothered to show still proved irritating.

The loud music drowned out the paparazzi-filled helicopters that circled overhead determined to grab their own personal view of history in the making, let alone the task of capturing footage and photos for the day job.

Most of the crowd below and beyond were unable to see their heroine in the flesh such was the position of the Rotunda's rooftop, but it didn't matter as people danced and sang to their favourite tunes which were being belted out live across the city. When fans heard an artist perform live it always seemed to radiate a special kind of immeasurable magic compared to a studio recording of the songs. However, so that the wide-spread crowds could still somehow visually become involved in the concert, huge TV screens had been stationed at Millennium Point, Victoria Square, the grounds of St Phillip's Cathedral in

Colmore Row and as far away as the Jewellery Quarter to radiate live images of the wonderful musical proceedings.

However, there was one entity in the vicinity that didn't fully appreciate the ground-breaking music on offer. Just a few floors down from the rooftop of the Rotunda, Mr. Mustard was burying his ears under his paws as the loud frequencies compromised his attempts at sleeping.

Nevertheless, Mr. Mustard's owner was enjoying himself immensely and Judd was honoured beyond comprehension when Phoenix actually took the time to dedicate her version of The Beatle's "Don't Let Me Down", which the Liverpool band had performed on their own rooftop gig, to her "very own Frank Farmer". Phoenix had followed up the dedication with a wink to the blushing Judd Stone.

Sadie and Yasmin were having a whale of a time dancing away to their heart's content with each given track, whilst Xanthe simply stood rooted to the spot tapping her left hand on her thigh to every single beat. The girl with Asperger's had her eyes transfixed on Phoenix absorbing every last detail of her idol's performance.

But all good things must come to an end and after some two and a half hours of incredible music, Phoenix finished her set before affectionately thanking the lovely people of Birmingham for helping her kickstart "The Wonderful World Tour". Due to the nature of it being a rooftop gig, she didn't provide an encore performance.

The streets of Birmingham were electric as the carnival atmosphere continued with fans chanting the lyrics to Phoenix's songs on their journeys home. Additionally, many people spilt into the many pubs on offer to continue their wonderful experience of the day.

Meanwhile, back on the rooftop, everyone was equally as thrilled at the success of the event.

"I'm going to check the news stream on my phone," said Sadie. "I want to know what's being said about the concert."

"There may even be a picture or video of us dancing," joked Yasmin, the good vibes of the concert had even been able to stifle her usual pessimism.

But Judd noticed a sudden and stark change in the expression on Sadie's face as she looked down at the screen of her phone.

"What's up, Sadie?" Judd asked with a new-found concern.

"It's Warwick."

"What about him?"

"It seems that he was being transferred between prisons when the van he was being carried in crashed on the M6."

"Is he dead?"

"Far from it. He's escaped from police custody and nobody knows where he is. You'd better keep an extra eye on Phoenix, Judd."

"And also on you, Sadie."

CHAPTER 25
THE MORNING AFTER

The next morning found Judd waking with a pounding head and Mr. Mustard licking at his face. "Ok, ok I'll feed you, boy. Just as soon as the room stops spinning." He lifted his head and immediately had to rest it back on the pillow as the disco that was booming in his head escalated with the movement. Then somehow, involving an admirable amount of will-power, Judd managed to slowly rise to the side of the bed and sit for a short while to compose himself whilst Mr. Mustard sat waiting obediently with his tail wagging. Judd winced knowing that the subsequent effort of trying to just stand up was going to be an almighty challenge following the effects of last night's partying.

The rooftop concert that had been staged on the Rotunda building had been an incredible success and to celebrate the occasion the inevitable 'rock and roll' proceedings had played out following the short and convenient trip to Judd's apartment.

For all the previous judgement he had held regarding Phoenix's lifestyle, last night Judd found himself indulging in heavy quantities of booze and cocaine as the excitement of the event seemed to suggest that anything and everything was ok. Even Neima had partaken in the frivolity, and drugs were definitely not her scene. But Judd discovered that the enchanting Phoenix can be a very persuasive lady when she wants to be, and great company to be in too when that twat Kaleb isn't around. Her infectious charisma made it difficult not to be drawn into her idea of fun.

Judd was glad that Phoenix had stayed at his apartment knowing that the useless Kaleb had gone AWOL and discovering that Warwick was at large. After all, his job was to protect her and even when he found himself intoxicated he knew she was at her safest being here in his Rotunda apartment with him.

The agony of standing upright subsided when he looked over at Neima who had once again shared his bed and he smiled as he watched her gently sleep. She was a beautiful person inside and out but neither of them was rushing to decide if they actually had a future together.

"Come on then, Mr. Mustard, lead me to the kitchen." The excited dog bounced ahead of his master.

Judd's apartment had two bedrooms. He slightly pushed the door open of bedroom number two to take a look on Phoenix and was a little taken aback to see the superstar snuzzled between both Sadie and Yasmin. He turned to Mr. Mustard in order to share his surprising discovery. "Wow! Last night it really did seem to be the theme that anything goes, boy."

Although Phoenix was technically dating Kaleb, she had never made a secret of her also finding girls attractive. It was part of Phoenix's DNA to push the boundaries of life, and that included having sex and sampling a variety of things with a diverse range of both men and women if she were to truly enjoy the richness of what life had to offer. Of course, he knew about Yasmin's preference of sexual partner, but Sadie? He had never guessed that one. He had assumed that she was heterosexual all the way. It seemed the three girls had simply got carried away with the occasion and made the most of it. And why not? The scene of the contented three girls before him was certainly more heartening than seeing Rodriguez or Stansfield in the bed.

Fortunately, Ben Francis had collected Xanthe not long after the concert and took her home safely. If Judd had allowed Xanthe to become within ten yards of drugs and alcohol he knew that Ben would have had his guts for garters.

Judd quietly closed the door to the bedroom so not to disturb the sleeping angels and continued his journey towards the kitchen. His head took another spin when he noticed that his living room looked as if a bomb had gone off in it. The rest of the band had simply fallen asleep where they finally collapsed and Judd couldn't escape noticing the telling trails of white powder spread along his smoked-glass occasional table. Scattered amongst the zombie-like bodies were scores of empty beer cans and various bottles of spirits. Rock and Roll had certainly come to the Rotunda last night. He was at least relieved to discover that his TV had not been pulled off the wall and thrown out of the window onto the pavement of the Bull Ring below. Judd was thankful that not all aspects of the cliché rock and roll lifestyle had been bestowed upon his home.

Dodging the obstacles of beer cans, bottles and even the odd item of removed clothing, including a very fetching lacy red bra that caught his eye, Judd eventually made it to the kitchen. He fed Mr. Mustard, gagging at the overwhelming stench of dog food which did little to ease his hangover, filled two glasses of water from the tap and once again skirted around the scattered mayhem of his flat to arrive back at his bed.

"Hey, Neima. I've got you some water, if you feel half as bad as I do you need re-hydrating girl."

Neima stirred and whispered a thank you before taking a couple of mouthfuls of the water. She handed the glass back to Judd and slumped back down onto the pillow. She had not opened her eyes once.

"So, I was right, you do feel as half as bad as I do."

Neima offered some kind of incoherent answer.

Judd sighed. "I've got some serious tidying up to do after last night."

"Don't worry, I'll help you," groaned Neima. "Later. Much later."

"It was a good night, Neima."

"It was a great night."

Judd lay back down next to Neima. Soon after he fell fast asleep.

CHAPTER 26
VIVA LAS VEGAS

Everyone on board cheered as Phoenix Easter's private jet landed on the runway of McCarran International Airport to the tune of Elvis's "Viva Las Vegas" over the plane's speaker system.

Judd had travelled sitting next to Neima, positioned just behind the seats that had been occupied by his close friends William Chamberlain and Crystal Stance. Due to his physical disabilities brought on by his MS, William had needed to sit at the front of the plane in order to easily receive assistance from the flight crew.

Also, on board were Sadie, Xanthe and Ben Francis. Much to her infuriation Yasmin hadn't travelled as she was required to assist in keeping the PI business afloat alongside Ted Armstrong. Besides someone needed to take care of Mr. Mustard while Judd wasn't around and Yasmin had been handed that responsibility too. Sab, who was going to meet her old friends along the Vegas strip was going to have to wait a little longer to see her little sister again.

Ocran la Boeuf hadn't travelled with them either which

seemed a little strange to Judd considering his star artist was about to take the USA by storm, but Neima and Phoenix had both stated that it made sense to them because he was always such a busy man. Nevertheless, Judd had a bad feeling about this guy. He still couldn't quite put his finger on it so he had asked Ted and Yasmin to check him out as a precautionary measure. After all, he was Phoenix's bodyguard now and he solely had her best interests at heart so he needed to be alert to any potential threat towards her no matter how obscure. Judd was determined that Phoenix would not become the next member of the infamous 27 Club.

Unfortunately, Kaleb Rodriguez had also travelled with the entourage. After his unexplained disappearing trick, he had resurfaced like the proverbial bad penny or bad smell, and Judd remained totally baffled as to why Phoenix allowed this waste of space anywhere in her life. Anyway, while the opportunity presented itself, there was no way Kaleb was going to miss out on an all-expenses-paid trip to the city of sin.

Neima noticed the shifting expressions on Judd's face. His features morphed from one of excitement to one of downheartedness. "It looks as though you didn't ask her to come along after all, did you?"

"Wrong. I asked her all right. She said no."

"Oh, Judd. I'm sorry," said Neima rubbing Judd's arm with compassion.

"It looks as though I really have lost Brooke forever, Neima. Even an amazing experience such as this wasn't enough to entice her to get within earshot of me. She must truly hate me for what I did to her."

"Look, forget about her for now. You're on a trip of a lifetime here so enjoy it. Besides, I need someone who I can bore to tears with my own pathetic love triangle don't I?"

"Still no joy for you in that department then?"

Neima shook her head. "No Judd and I can never tell

the person how I feel?"

"Well, he's missing out for sure the poor bastard. You're a wonderful woman, Neima. I don't think I've ever met anyone as warm and as kind as you. Why not just tell him, he'll probably be over the moon and snap your arm off for a relationship with you."

Neima smiled. "Who said it's a he?"

Judd was consumed with awkwardness. "Oh, I see. You're in love with a woman? Sorry I just assumed…"

"Don't worry it's an easy mistake to make and I have kept you guessing."

"Well in my defence, I do know from personal experience that you certainly know your way around a man's body, Neima."

"You'll make me blush, Judd. You know, I did actually seriously consider making my feelings for her known on this trip, but only for one crazy minute and then that idiot decides to turn up in her life again anyway."

Judd's jaw dropped. "Oh my God! It's Phoenix isn't it?"

"I told you it was complicated. Sometimes you can't choose who you fall for, it just happens. I can never tell her, Judd. It would make too many things implode. I have to think about managing her career too."

"Wow, I can see why it's complicated. Oh well, you have me as a friend for this little trip, Neima."

"A friend with benefits too. I'm not complaining."

"And I'll keep a close eye on that Muppet, Kaleb. If he puts Phoenix in any danger just once I'm going to break his legs."

"You'll have to get in line behind me first, Hun."

Judd managed a smile. But he was also mindful that in addition to Kaleb supplying potentially harmful amounts of drugs to Phoenix left, right and centre, Warwick Stansfield was also still at large. Stansfield could pose a threat to both Phoenix and Sadie, one of the reasons why he had asked his little friend from the University coffee shop along so he could also keep a protective eye over her too.

It seemed less likely that Stansfield would turn up in Las Vegas, but Judd was also constantly aware that Phoenix was to celebrate her 27th birthday while in Vegas and that presented a very real problem in its own right. There was no doubt that she was typically going to party in style for her 27th birthday and she was going to party hard. Her choice of lifestyle could be viewed as being self-destructive and one which seriously places her at harm, never mind any posh-boy psychos being on the loose that are also gunning for her.

The birthday celebrations were to take place amongst a couple of weeks gigging at Caesar's Palace before Phoenix performed the Mother of all concerts at the Grand Canyon. Implementing the necessary security arrangements was going to be tough.

Judd Stone's mission was simple: to ensure that Phoenix Easter did not become the next member of the 27 club.

.

CHAPTER 27
THE UNEXPECTED ARRIVAL

Phoenix had so far played three back to back concerts at Caesar's Palace to three very appreciative crowds. In terms of bodyguard duties, for Judd, there had been no cause for concern. He was able to relax and enjoy the shows, complete with Phoenix's rapturous encores, and just like what he had observed on the rooftop of the Rotunda building he marvelled at how well Phoenix was able to perform in spite of her wild lifestyle.

By now LAPD's Sabita Mistry had arrived and hooked up with her friends once again. Today she had joined them to wander along the Las Vegas Strip and the Nevada sun was blistering hot as it beamed down on the happy gathering. The heat was enjoyable compared to the typical British weather, however, the blast of air-conditioning with each and every incredible hotel complex that they visited was more than welcoming to ease the uncomfortable sweats.

Judd, Sab and the devoted Crystal had all offered to ferry William around Las Vegas in his wheelchair until he reminded them that he had arranged for a powered mobility scooter to be provided. The deluxe model was very 'bling', gold in colour and possessed more mirrors than a Mod's Lambretta. The scooter had provided a number of opportunities for friendly banter, mainly between Judd and William.

Neima and Sadie had also joined them, while Ben and Xanthe had broken away temporarily to catch a magic show. Xanthe was able to provide a running commentary to her uncle about how the magic tricks were performed, such was her incredible ability to decipher the illusions as they unfolded.

Phoenix and Kaleb had been left sleeping in the hotel. Neither Judd nor Neima wanted Kaleb around Phoenix, he was a bad influence on an already vulnerable and impulsive individual, but in truth what could be done about the situation? Phoenix was a grown woman who made her own decisions and if she wanted Kaleb around then that was that. Judd made sure that he was discreetly monitoring the situation though. He didn't like Kaleb and he didn't trust him. The moment that he put a foot wrong was going to be his last.

Turning left once leaving Caesar's Palace, the group had first visited The Mirage, where Judd had purchased a number of items from The Beatles Shop and had vowed to catch a showing of Cirque Du Soleil's 'Love' before the trip to Las Vegas was over.

Eventually, Judd was persuaded to vacate the Mirage hotel complex which paid tribute to his all-time favourite musicians and not long after the friends were enjoying a gondola ride on the mimicked waterways of Venice at The Venetian Hotel. The Gondolier was amazed once Judd had informed him that his hometown of Birmingham, England could actually boast more waterways than Venice.

A short-lived Poker game in Harrah's, which had resulted in Neima being the only victor from the group (both Crystal and Sadie had only watched the games unable to grasp the rules), at least secured a free lunch for everyone else.

"What are you going to spend that small profit on?" Crystal had asked Neima.

"I'm going to treat all of my new-found friends to lunch."

"You should treat yourself to something nice," said Sab. "You've earned it."

"No way, come on let's head up to Paris. It's my treat." This was a typical unselfish act of kindness by Neima. Everyone thanked her and headed up to the Paris themed Las Vegas Hotel.

But as they slipped under the hotel's trademark model of a hot-air balloon and the mock Eiffel Tower, Judd suddenly lost his appetite for food and had instead built up a thirst for gambling now that he had tasted it at the previous encounters.

"You guys carry on, I'm going to have a go at Crap."

"Too much information, Judd. But if you want to make a little room for your meal we can wait for you to go to the toilet."

"That's not what he means, Neima," said William sour-faced. Neima looked confused. "He wants to play a game of Crap instead of taking you up on your kind offer of lunch. I knew it was a mistake to start gambling."

"Relax, William. Just one game or two and then I'll come and join you," said Judd.

"Judd, I know you too well. If you start with a win you'll continue believing you're on a winning streak, and if you lose you'll just keep trying to win thinking the next game you'll be lucky, followed by the next and the next and the next. Leave it alone, Judd."

"Stop being such a killjoy, William. Drop the lecture, won't you?"

"William is just looking out for you, Judd," said Crystal.

"Well, I tell you what Crystal, why don't you join me and you can predict how I'm going to do."

Crystal remained calm. "It doesn't quite work like that,

Judd, and you know it."

"There's no need for sarcasm, Judd. Now I said leave it." William was becoming increasingly impatient with his friend.

"This is really irritating, remind me when you became my dad, William."

"I'm just looking out for you like I have always done."

"Oh really? Well, where were you when I was getting sacked from the CID? Where were you when I was having to menace money out of honest people for the local gangster?"

"My God, you'll be asking me to wipe your arse next."

"Really? What, when you can hardly manage to wipe your own?"

Everyone fell into an awkward silence. Judd instantly knew that he had overstepped the mark and regretted his jibe at William. It was incredible how childish he had become.

"Hey, William. I'm sorry. I didn't mean that."

"I know you didn't. You felt under pressure, and do you know why? Because you're an addict. Addicts always do things they don't mean because it's the addiction that warps their personality and drives them to do irrational things, just to feed the habit. You're addicted to gambling. I thought you had kicked the habit but now I'm not so sure. You're right Judd, I haven't been around much, I was foolish enough to think that I had a life to lead and to grab a little happiness with Crystal with the time I have left, and to be honest, each day I'm on this earth feels as though it could be my last. But you know what, you've actually done fine without me. You've turned your life around without my help. You're the bodyguard to the world's most famous pop star for Christ's sake! I'm proud of you so don't fuck it all up now for the sake of a shit game of crap – pun totally intended."

Judd looked to the ceiling and ran his fingers through his hair before speaking. "I'm not addicted to gambling."

"So, prove it. Come to lunch with us and don't take part in another minute of gambling the whole time we're in Vegas."

Judd turned away from his friend, while the remainder of the gathering waited in anticipation. He stared at the Crap table and then back at his friend. The temptation was strong. William also stared at the Crap table and his own temptation surfaced: to use his telekinetic powers to toss the table into the air creating mayhem and putting an end to any further gambling in that vicinity. But he resisted. This had to be Judd's choice and the choice would be another momentous step taken by his closest friend.

"Come on, Judd. Please, come with us," said Sab, who was broken-hearted at seeing her two old friends at each other's throats.

"I will, Sab. I will."

"Right now?" she continued.

He looked at Neima, she hadn't said a word not seeing it as her place. However, the expression in her eyes begged him to come to lunch and leave the Crap game alone. That look should have been enough to convince him what to do but the temptation remained strong. Anyway, what difference would one lousy game make?

"Ok, I've made my decision."

Just then the moment was halted as he looked once again at Neima but then seemed to look beyond her, over her shoulder.

"My decision is, I'm coming to lunch. Of course, I am, sorry you guys…But can you also make room for one more?"

One more? The party were confused.

The confusion subsided when Judd was greeted by a familiar woman who broke through the crowd and hugged him tightly.

"At last I've found you. Once I couldn't find you at Caesar's Palace I thought that was my chance gone."

"Brooke, what are you doing here?"

"I've tried hating you, Judd Stone but I can't. You're a complete bastard but I miss you like crazy. So, if you still want me around here I am."

Judd hugged Brooke once more. He couldn't believe this was happening, his deep-rooted love for Brooke had never gone away. He caught a glimpse at Neima wondering how she might react. She had always known about Brooke but considering their friendship, which was one with clear benefits, he wondered was he being a little insensitive for the second time in only a couple of minutes. But this time the look in Neima's eyes was one of understanding which was accompanied by a friendly smile.

Judd broke away from hugging Brooke. "Brooke, I want you to meet a very special lady. This is Neima."

The two women amicably shook hands.

"Neima is Phoenix's manager and a truly wonderful person and a very dear friend."

"Well any friend of Judd's is a friend of mine, just ask these guys," said Brooke moving her hand along the line of people. "I'm sure you're swell too," she said acknowledging Sadie once their eyes met for the first time. Sadie returned a smile.

"I'm very pleased to meet you, Brooke. I've heard a lot about you from Judd," said Neima.

"All good I hope?"

"All good, I promise. I'm about to treat this little gang to lunch, please join us."

"Thanks, Neima, I will."

The meal was delicious. Judd and William put their spat to bed and everyone left Paris Las Vegas many hours later as they laughed and drank and drank and laughed into the night.

It was fortunate that Phoenix had a break from performing tonight because none of them were in any kind of state to accomplish their supporting duties.

CHAPTER 28
THE DOUBLE WEDDING

"You may kiss the brides," said Elvis Presley.

Two very English men in the form of Judd Stone and William Chamberlain had just engaged in a very American wedding, well a very Las Vegas wedding anyhow. Their deep-rooted bond had enabled them to settle their temporary differences with ease and each had been selected by the other to be the best man for their respective wedding.

The brides, who both looked stunning on their special day, had each been walked down the aisle and given away by another conjured-up form of Elvis, and following the kissing of the brides the impersonators had expertly burst into song with the King's hit "Can't Help Falling In Love".

The most generous and amazing wedding gift then followed as Phoenix teamed up with the 'Elvi' to sing "The Wonder Of You", "Burning Love" and an ironic rendition of "The Girl Of My Best Friend". Everyone howled at the choice of song as the lyrics unfurled. Phoenix had even made an effort to wear a version of the King's iconic white jumpsuit which he had sported for his concerts at the International Hotel all those years ago.

Fortunately, although clearly a snub, Kaleb had failed to show at the occasion in order to offer his congratulations. His absence pleased Judd no end.

William, whose physical health remained a concern, had achieved his goal of standing throughout the ceremony symbolising a very successful event for the wedded couples of Mr. William and Mrs. Crystal Chamberlain and Mr. Judd and Mrs. Brooke Stone.

The couples had very different arrangements for the next few days. The Chamberlains were going to head down to Flagstaff to take in a mini-honeymoon and engage in a flight over the Grand Canyon. This would take them into the area for Phoenix's open-air concert at the wondrous site well ahead of schedule.

Judd meanwhile still had his duties to contend with in Las Vegas, not least attending Phoenix's 27th birthday bash which filled him with mixed emotions. It was going to be the mother of all parties and no doubt one like he had never experienced before, but as Phoenix was turning 27 this presented the very real concern that she could soon be meeting her maker. The potential for that to happen would no doubt escalate with the way Phoenix would intend to party. Even harder than ever before.

The party wasn't really the Chamberlain's scene so they agreed to meet up again when all parties arrived in Arizona.

The happy gathering moved outside the Elvis themed chapel with Sab and Neima being the first to scatter the guitar-shaped confetti.

The photographer continued to click away, and of course, unlike these two very lucky couples, not everyone could boast to having both Elvis Presley and Phoenix Easter in their wedding photos.

"You look truly beautiful, Brooke."

"You do too, Crystal. It was a great wedding wasn't it?"

"I honestly can't think of how we could have done it

any better."

Judd and William hugged one another in the same manner that the closest of brothers would have done.

"So, we are both finally honest men, mate," said Judd.

"I'm not sure you can quite claim that one, boys" joked Brooke ear-wigging.

Judd and William laughed along with her.

"Listen, you both enjoy Flagstaff. The flight over the Grand Canyon will be really something else. Brooke and I will catch up with you in a few days." As Judd spoke a pink Cadillac pulled into the courtyard. "So, this is how you're travelling into Arizona?"

"I thought Crystal would appreciate the continuation of classiness, or tackiness, they seem much the same thing in Vegas."

"Hey buddy, it's all part of making memories."

"You're right, and us two getting married to our ladies together like this. It's a great memory isn't it, Judd?"

"The best, buddy. The best."

"I think we had them crying in the chapel."

Judd laughed. "Very good, I saw what you did there. Just don't sing and ruin this wonderful day will you mate? I reckon your singing voice would even make it rain in Vegas. To tell you the truth, I'm close to tears myself but don't let on."

"Far be it from me to compromise the street cred of Judd Stone."

Not long after Judd and Brooke waved their friends goodbye as the Pink Cadillac pulled away.

Suddenly Phoenix appeared at their side.

"Hey Phoenix, thanks for joining in the singing back there, it really added to the occasion. The jumpsuit looks great by the way."

"Yes, thanks Phoenix, we will always be extremely grateful to you," echoed Brooke.

"It was my pleasure. Actually, I really enjoyed singing those songs, I may slip one of them into my set for the tour. By the way, I hope your friends like their Cadillac, Judd."

"Their Cadillac? I thought William had hired it?"

"I've just let him think that for a while. The chauffeur will have informed the Chamberlains of their gift by the time they reach Flagstaff."

"You bought it for them?" said Judd, more than a little surprised. "Wow, that's really generous of you. Them old Cadillac's are worth a fortune in that condition."

"Well, I hope that you and Brooke like yours too. Here it comes now."

Both Judd and Brooke's jaws dropped to the floor as a white Cadillac with its roof down pulled up next to them.

"Phoenix, I don't know what to say?" said a bowled-over Judd.

"Well we couldn't have an Elvis themed wedding without the happy couple getting a Cadillac a la Elvis style, now could we? I guess as the bonafide singer of the occasion I took the liberty to step into Mr. Presley's shoes to bear gifts in the shape of a Cadillac just as he would have done."

"Phoenix, I honestly don't believe that we can ever thank you enough," said an indebted Brooke.

"Seeing the smiles on yours and Judd's faces is more than enough for me, Brooke. Now you two make sure that you go and have a happy life together."

Judd turned to his gorgeous bride. "Well Mrs. Stone, it seems that we now have a surefire method presented to us to escape this little lot and be chauffeured somewhere appropriate in order for us to consummate our marriage?"

Without hesitation, Brooke Stone stepped into the rear of the Cadillac. "Well come on Stud, jump in. What are you waiting for? And who said anything about being appropriate?"

Judd Stone was in the back of that long car quicker than you could say blue suede shoes.

CHAPTER 29
THE BLACK DOG

"Are you crying," asked Yasmin bluntly as she burst through the door.

Ted Armstrong hurried away his box of tissues into the drawer of the desk and composed himself as best he could.

"Sorry, Yasmin. You shouldn't have to see me like that."

"Don't apologise, dude. What's up?"

"You don't want to hear about my troubles."

"Try me, a problem shared and all that. We're partners now aren't we? Sort of anyway."

Ted felt like crying all over again. He was truly touched to discover that Yasmin actually had a heart after all.

"It's nothing. I just get down sometimes."

Intuitively Mr. Mustard whined and placed his head affectionately on Ted's lap. Ted stroked the big head of the dog as Mr. Mustard's sad eyes looked up at the Private Investigator's teary face.

"Well, it doesn't seem like nothing. That's a shame that you get down sometimes. Why is that? Let me help if I can."

"It's how I got into the job really, that's the ironic thing. The love of my life cheated on me a few years back. He was very good at covering his tracks, but I knew he was up to something. When I finally caught him with another man he hit me repeatedly and twisted the situation to make out I was some kind of possessive stalker. The funny thing was I'd have forgiven him for what he'd done but he dumped me there and then. The black dog's been scratching at my door ever since."

"Mr. Mustard's not black?"

Ted allowed himself a smile. "Depression. I suffer from depression. It's sometimes referred to as the black dog."

"Oh really. I didn't know that."

"I've had counselling before now and the medication helps but clearly I still have bad days. You must think I'm pathetic."

"Not at all… Well, maybe just a little bit."

They laughed together.

"That's better. You have a nice smile, Ted, you should smile more often."

"You're quite a sweet girl really aren't you Yasmin."

"Don't tell everyone, I've got my reputation to think of."

"Your secret's safe, partner."

"You said he. I didn't realise you were gay, Ted."

"Why would you? I guess we've never really spoken much before, other than about work."

"Well let's change that right now shall we Ted? Let's get to know one another a little better and swap notes on our respective failed gay relationships."

"What do you have in mind?"

"Let's shut up shop and head on down to Hurst Street. We can get drunk while we chat things through."

"But there's all this paperwork to do."

"And doing lots of paperwork is going to lift your mood is it?"

"Not likely."

"And let's not forget that Judd and the others, including my own flaming sister, are living the high life in Las Vegas while we hold the fort here in rain-drenched Birmingham. I'm sure they wouldn't begrudge us engaging in a team building session under the circumstances."

"Team building? We have a team of two!" Mr. Mustard whined dejectedly. "Oh, sorry boy, of course, we have a team of three for sure, but dogs can't go in many of the pubs and bars down the Gay Village."

"Oh, I don't know. I've seen quite a few. In fact, I think I've snogged most of them."

Ted laughed. Actually, he had always been quite fond of Yasmin since the day they had met. He had never been put off by her surly nature like many others who met her. He found it quite an entertaining trait of hers, and besides, just as she was proving today he always knew she was a decent sort deep down. Ted had always sensed that despite her air of self-importance she would actually be one of those few people who could be relied upon when the chips were down. "You're on, Yasmin. Let's do it. I could do with a decent chat… and the odd pint."

"The odd pint? Scrub that, Ted. We're going to have champagne."

"Champagne? What are we celebrating?"

"I don't know yet, let's get drunk and work it out."

That really made Ted smile.

From that moment on an unlikely friendship began to blossom.

CHAPTER 30
THE BIRTHDAY PARTY

As one celebration ended in the pubs of Birmingham's Gay Village, so began another one thousands of miles away across the oceans. Today was the day that Phoenix Easter turned 27. It was certainly a day to celebrate but equally, for the likes of Neima, Xanthe and Judd, it was a time for concern as the superstar was now entering that potentially fatal year where so many artists before her had shuffled off their mortal coil.

Phoenix herself was fully aware of the significance of the year that her life was entering but she simply wasn't fussed. The manner in which she was celebrating tonight clearly underlined that she was still hellbent on pushing the boundaries of life and there was no intention of ever diminishing her indulgence in sex, drugs and rock and roll.

Under Phoenix's guidance, Neima had arranged all of the preparations and facilities that were required for the official birthday party, including entertainment, bedroom suites, food and alcohol, whilst the ever-generous Phoenix had insisted on picking up the entire bill as a treat for all of her friends.

CLUB 27

As it happened the celebrations had typically started way before the birthday party had officially begun with a pub crawl involving a close-knit gathering of Phoenix's friends around Downtown Vegas and along the hotel bars of the Las Vegas Strip.

Judd, being a seasoned drinker, knew that unlike many others he could match Phoenix drink for drink, and she encouraged him to do so, but he ensured that with every fourth drink that he had he replaced a beer with a litre of water. Judd knew that he was amidst the party celebrations of his lifetime and he was keen to take advantage and enjoy himself, but he also knew he had a job to do and refused to ever consider himself off duty. He needed to balance the fun with a great deal of vigilance in case anything untoward happened towards this very special birthday girl. In particular, Judd scanned every inch of every location they frequented just in case an out-of-place individual carrying an umbrella was lurking about. Additionally, it was not beyond the realms of possibility for Warwick Stansfield to appear either, Judd refused to take for granted that the posh-boy psycho was most likely thousands of miles away.

Judd had noticed Phoenix's many trips to the bathroom, incidentally in tandem with Kaleb, and he quickly realised that the use of the toilet facilities was not necessarily due to the plentiful intake of liquid. The telltale signs of snorting cocaine were evident with each and every bathroom visit as Phoenix's excitability increased and her pupils became more and more dilated. Besides, the most recent trip provided a full-on view of a gathering of white powder which nestled on the tip of her nose. Phoenix giggled as Judd used a napkin to wipe away the evidence, an intrusive act in the eyes of Kaleb which didn't seem to please the superstar's boyfriend – not that Judd cared what the parasite thought for even a nano-second.

Once the early-starters eventually arrived at Phoenix's official birthday party, Judd found that he could relax a little. The hotel's own security personnel were working admirably to ensure that only those with official tickets were allowed access to the party and therefore the appearance of a stranger holding an umbrella was very unlikely.

Another round of shots was delivered to the table courtesy of Phoenix's generosity and Judd's and Phoenix's eyes met as they were typically the first to finish downing the sour liquid.

Just then the duetted track by George Michael and Whitney Houston "If I Told You That" blasted over the sound system.

"So, Frank Farmer, I wanna dance with somebody."

"Do you really?" asked Judd smiling.

"Yes, I do and I want it to be with my big, strong, protective bodyguard. Come on, Judd. Come and dance with me."

Judd turned to Brooke who just shrugged and said: "Go ahead."

Phoenix stood up and took a step towards Judd. "I want to dance with my very own bodyguard at my very own birthday party."

"Well, in that case, how could I possibly refuse? It would be a pleasure to dance with you, Miss Easter," and with that Judd reached out and took Phoenix's hand ready to lead her to the dancefloor.

But not everyone was as relaxed as Brooke Stone about the situation.

"Let go of my girlfriend's hand, Stone. Who do you think you are?"

Judd turned to Kaleb but decided to simply ignore the remark, shake his head in irritation and turn away from the possessive boyfriend.

Judd and Phoenix had taken all but two steps towards the dancefloor when Kaleb had managed to jump up and manoeuvre in front of them succeeding in blocking their path. It was quite an achievement considering the amount of alcohol and drugs that he too had taken.

Phoenix tutted which couldn't be heard over the sublime vocals of George and Whitney. "Kaleb, what are you doing? Get out of the way, I want to dance," she said.

"Then dance with me instead of this testosterone filled dickhead."

"Just what is your problem, Kaleb?" said Judd.

"You're my fucking problem, Stone. You swan around all the time like you're some kind of tough guy and then right in front of my very eyes you have the audacity to grab my girl's hand."

"You need to chill, mate. All those narcotics are making you paranoid," quipped Judd.

"Kaleb, I pay Judd to be a tough guy. I need protection," said Phoenix.

"And that probably includes protection from you," said Judd, unable to help himself.

"Are you going to let him talk to me like that, babe?" said Kaleb staring manically at Phoenix through dilated pupils.

"I'll tell you what, Kaleb. I'll tread on his toes while we're dancing, how's that?"

"Don't make fun of me, Phoenix."

"Then stop being such a dickhead, Kaleb."

Kaleb was incensed at his girlfriend's tone. He promptly squared up closer to Phoenix and grabbed at her face, squeezing her cheeks hard. "Don't talk to me like that babes."

Instinctively Judd grabbed Kaleb's offending arm and within seconds he had it held behind Kaleb's back, causing the jealous boyfriend a considerable amount of pain.

"You know, it was that type of move that had your cousin on his arse and got me employed in the first place, Rodriguez."

"No, Judd. Don't hurt him," begged Phoenix. Judd failed to understand why she would bother to do so.

"Ok, ok man I'm cool," groaned a pathetic Kaleb.

"It's ok, Judd. The song has finished now anyway," said Phoenix.

Nothing would have given Judd more pleasure at that precise moment in time than to break Kaleb's arm there and then, but reluctantly he released his grip on the lowlife and allowed him to scurry back to his seat. He turned to face Phoenix who had quietly started to cry.

"You can do so much better than that joker, Phoenix. He's no good for you. I really don't know what you see in him."

"I'll second that," shouted Neima.

Phoenix wiped away a tear. "He loves me and I love him, it's as simple as that."

"He has a funny way of showing it," shouted Neima again.

"You shut your mouth," shouted Kaleb towards Neima.

"I suggest that you shut yours," countered Judd aggressively.

Kaleb realised that it was in his best interest to comply with Judd's instruction, but a sulky look proceeded to dominate his face.

Phoenix took a deep breath and with all the muster of the true professional that she was she managed to compose herself remarkably well. On the outside at least. "Right you lot. This is my birthday party and I want us all to get along and carry on enjoying the night. Right Neima?"

"Right." Neima raised a glass to underline her commitment.

"Judd?"

"No problem."

"Kaleb?"

Kaleb failed to answer, still sulking like a schoolboy.

"Right Kaleb?"

"Right."

"Ok, then. That's better and we are all in agreement."

Phoenix grabbed the attention of a waitress who was cruising nearby. "Another round of shots here please, Honey."

"Sure thing, I'll bring them over as quick as I can."

"Thank you." Phoenix returned her attention to the people before her. "Now come on everyone, lighten up. This is supposed to be a fucking party and it also happens to be my fucking party. Help me make it a night to remember."

CHAPTER 31
THE JIMI HENDRIX EXPERIENCE

"Help! Somebody help, she's not breathing."

Judd was woken suddenly by Kaleb's frantic screams. He and Brooke had fallen asleep the night before on the large sofa that was nestled in the lounging area of Phoenix's luxury suite. The suite was so large, many of the partygoers had simply crashed down in a suitable spot of their choosing or literally fallen asleep where they had dropped due to the intake of alcohol and narcotics.

Judd leapt up from the sofa and rushed to Phoenix's bedroom, clearing a couple of stirring bodies on the way as if he were an Olympic hurdler. The scene that welcomed him was Phoenix lying motionless on her back, eyes closed and with streams of vomit running down either side of her mouth. Kaleb was futilely kneeling over her with his hands on his head and crying like a baby.

Judd concluded that there was no time for pleasantries and pushed Kaleb out of the way so that he could access Phoenix's seemingly lifeless body, quickly realising that she must have choked on her own vomit. He turned her onto her stomach and promptly used the palm of his hand to strike five swift blows in between her shoulder blades in an attempt to free anything that was wedged in her throat and to set her breathing again. Phoenix didn't respond.

"She's dead, she's dead," wailed Kaleb, offering nothing constructive to actually benefit the situation at all.

"Shut up, Kaleb," shouted Judd. "You're not helping matters."

Judd now decided to turn Phoenix onto her side and he placed his fingers in her mouth in a desperate attempt to free her airways. His fingers prodded and searched the mouth that had been responsible for releasing the most beautiful of singing voices, and eventually, Judd managed to successfully remove a multitude of clogged debris.

Disturbingly, Phoenix remained motionless.

"Come on Phoenix, don't you do a Jimi Hendrix on me girl," said Judd, desperate to see some sign of life from the rock star.

Next, he moved behind Phoenix and lifted her limp body and he feared the worst as she lifelessly flopped forward. Judd wrapped his arms around her stomach, making a fist with one hand and placing the other hand over it to secure a hug from behind. Phoenix continued to flop over his embrace. He pulled his hands inwards and upwards, pressing sharply into Phoenix's stomach just above her pierced belly button. After five or so attempts of squeezing Phoenix, she opened her eyes with a large gasp and projectile vomited across the room. She followed this with three less volatile vomiting episodes, but importantly she was breathing and she was alive.

By now Neima had entered the room and she headed straight for the babbling mess sitting on the floor striking him repeatedly about the head. "This is all your fault, she nearly died because of you and the shit that you feed into her system."

"Fuck off, leave me alone" screamed Kaleb raising his arms above his head in a vain attempt to try and protect himself, but Neima continued her vicious assault.

Meanwhile, Phoenix sat down on the bed, her eyes widened and she looked dazed and shocked.

"Are you, ok?" asked Judd. Phoenix simply nodded.

Judd moved his attention towards the one-sided conflict taking place across the room, and although he too would find enormous pleasure in hurting Kaleb, he did the decent thing and pulled Neima away from the low-life.

"Come on Neima, he's not worth dirtying your hands on."

Somehow, managing to take notice of Judd through the thick red mist of anger, Neima turned her attention away from Kaleb and ran to Phoenix, squeezing her nearly as hard as Judd had done moments earlier. She was totally unperturbed by the amount of sick that she was rubbing against whilst hugging the woman she loved.

"Oh Phoenix, I thought we'd lost you."

Completely out of character, Phoenix began to cry.

CHAPTER 32
THE CONVERSATION

Judd was sitting in Phoenix's hotel suite once more whilst the superstar showered in a nearby room. He was reading a Peter James novel and was enjoying doing so. Brooke had decided to partake in some serious clothes shopping with Sab and Sadie, whilst the workaholic Neima was in her own hotel room keeping the business side of the Phoenix brand ticking over. The unpopular Kaleb had announced that he was popping out for a 'bit of business' which most likely meant he was out to score some drugs.

As he reached the end of his chapter he could hear that Phoenix had killed the water in the shower followed by the sound of the cubicle door swinging open. Soon after Phoenix appeared wearing a bathrobe and towel wrapped around her hair.

"Here, I've made you a cup of English tea," said Phoenix as Judd gratefully accepted the mug. "I left it brewing while I had a shower."

Phoenix looked stunning even without a hint of makeup or her hair hanging down, but Judd knew as she sat down opposite him her lack of clothing was not a 'come-on' to him in any shape or form. Judd never thought of her in that way, he had a job to do, he was just her bodyguard and that was that. Of course, there wasn't a man on earth who didn't find Phoenix Easter attractive, but Judd and Phoenix's association had grown to become more like a brother and sister relationship, Judd being the older brother of course.

Judd possessed an overpowering desire to protect his star employer and not only because he was duty-bound because of his occupation. Judd believed that Phoenix was vulnerable, not least because she was in a relationship with a toxic lowlife called Kaleb Rodriguez. Judd was also acutely conscious that Phoenix fitted the profile of a star that could die at the age of 27, like many before her, and become the next member of the cursed 27 club. Almost choking to death on her own vomit had been a stark reminder to that. But regardless of Phoenix seemingly fitting the 27 club profile, Judd, of course, possessed a deep-rooted guilt in his subconscious mind and a compelling feeling of responsibility to protect the women who entered his life. This strong feeling of responsibility coupled with a sensitivity of being inadequate was born out of the tragic events surrounding the deaths of his first wife Frankie, who was murdered by a released prisoner whom he had been responsible for locking up, and early girlfriend Bonnie, who had committed suicide following a rape that he felt he could have prevented. These tragic deaths would always ensure that he would be cautiously protective of any female placed in his care.

"You look like you want to talk," said Judd closing his book and placing the bookmark between the pages.

Phoenix curled her bare legs under her and took a sip from her mug of tea which she always grasped with both hands.

"Well, it's about time I thanked you isn't it?"

"For what?"

"For saving my life you numpty."

"I was just doing my job."

"Oh, really? I don't recall noticing that performing the Heimlich Manoeuvre and clearing airways of rotting vomit being included in your job spec."

"Very poetically put. I can see now why you're such a successful songwriter."

Phoenix laughed which provided the opportunity to once again reveal her trademark gold tooth.

"I noted Kaleb wasn't half as helpful," said Phoenix, surprising Judd somewhat. She was usually quite quick to defend her man.

"Let's just say he panicked a little, shall we?"

"He panicked a lot, I'd say. He was fucking useless."

"Kaleb is fucking useless, Phoenix. Full stop. Forgive me but you could do so much better for yourself."

"So, I keep being told. But we love each other. It's that simple. I don't walk around blind, Judd. I know he pisses people off and I haven't forgotten he was a dickhead the night we wanted to dance either. Yes, I know that he can be a complete dickhead but you can't choose who you fall for."

"I guess so. Anyway, how do you know he was so useless? You were unconscious. Ahh, I guess Neima filled you in."

"She didn't have to."

"I don't follow."

"I saw it all."

"I definitely don't follow."

"I know I can speak to you about this, Judd. Your friend, Crystal is a psychic medium, right? So, I know your mind has been opened to lots of possibilities of things we don't necessarily understand."

Judd was intrigued. "Go on."

"I saw it all, Judd. I saw myself choking on the vomit. I saw myself stop breathing and I saw Kaleb acting hysterically."

"Wow, you had an out of body experience?"

"I certainly did."

"It couldn't have been a reaction to the drugs, making you hallucinate."

Phoenix rolled her eyes. "Do me a favour."

"Sorry. That was dumb of me."

"I saw it all so vividly, Judd. I was hovering over my own lifeless body and then a light appeared, it was so peaceful and I felt compelled to walk towards it. I knew there and then that if I entered the light there'd be no turning back but the feeling of peacefulness and stability that was calling me was overwhelming. But then I saw you grab hold of me and to be frank, the effort that you went to in saving me just couldn't go unrewarded, so I simply decided now is not my time and I was back in the room."

"Bloody hell, that's amazing."

"Isn't it. But I do fear my time is nigh, Judd."

"What makes you say that, you're only 27 years old."

"Exactly. Don't you think that I'm also acutely aware of the 27 club? Some of my greatest inspirations are members of that damn club. And I'm not that dumb to know people are surmising that I could be next, including you no doubt, Judd. Especially with how it's perceived that Kaleb pumps me full of drugs."

"Well, he doesn't seem to help matters."

"People need to realise I make my own choices. I enjoy the drugs, that's why I take them. Kaleb is just a victim of circumstance."

"Are you sure that it's not the other way around. I fear Kaleb is a bad influence on you, Phoenix. You could get clean without him. He makes you do too much of it. I've seen him in action."

"I saw Neima in action too, she clearly agrees with you."

Judd laughed. "Yeah, I thought I was going to have to save his life as well as yours the way she was steaming into him. She has a point though, Neima."

"Can we move the subject away from Kaleb, please,"

Phoenix inadvertently gave a puppy dog eyes look over the top of her mug as she sipped her tea which ensured that Judd would be unable to resist complying with her request.

"Yeah sure. Let me just say this though. If you can tone down the drugs then they won't get their next member of the 27 club."

"I'm not sure it's lifestyle, Judd, that forces that membership to happen. I think it's destiny. Nothing can be done to prevent the death at age 27 if you're destined to become a member."

"Why do you say that?"

"Everyone peaks in their career, Judd. Even the stars with unrivalled longevity in the business still peaked at one time or another. So, when you're a certain type of star and you have reached the pinnacle of what you are to achieve it makes sense that you actually bow out."

"What do you mean? Like, go out on a high?"

"Exactly. Or go out when *high*. Think about it. The record companies know that when one of their artists dies all of their back catalogues gets resurrected and they make a final small fortune out of their dead star."

"That's a very cynical way of looking at things, Phoenix."

"But the basis of many conspiracy theories. When I've done this world tour and played gigs at the Grand Canyon and the like what is left for me to achieve? I'll have drawn my line in the sand and in doing so perhaps triggered my untimely death sentence."

"Blimey, you're almost as clued up as Xanthe?"

"The girl with Asperger's?"

"Yeah, she's an expert on the 27 Club and another of us who worries you could become a member."

"Aww, bless her. She's a sweet kid."

"There's loads of good music left in you yet, Phoenix."

"Maybe, maybe not. But undoubtedly, I will have peaked in my twenty-seventh year. If I die I'll be forever 27 won't I with a back catalogue of music that never had the opportunity to turn sour?"

"I never realised you thought like this, Phoenix."

"You may call me cynical, Judd, but is none of this theory connecting with you? It makes a certain kind of sense doesn't it?"

Judd had to agree but chose to look away rather than find the words to make his agreement a reality.

"Well, I'm here to protect you so I'm determined that you will make it to at least 28 and then you can never be a part of this damn 27 club circus."

"I know you'll give it your best shot, Judd. However, destiny may come calling either naturally or through the callous makings of others, but I won't join it by my own hand, Judd. Not like they think anyway…"

I won't join it by my own hand. Not like they think. What on earth had Phoenix meant by that remark? Judd didn't have time to contemplate the comment any further as he continued to be drawn into Phoenix's captivating conversation, even if the topic was making him feel a little uncomfortable at times. "… I certainly won't be selling my soul and offering myself as a blood sacrifice in my twenty-seventh year. I don't think any of the others did either. These artists were genuinely born talented. End of. They didn't have help from the Devil or anything else in order to be so artistically gifted, it's a disgrace to their memory to suggest such a thing. However, it can't be denied that the fascination surrounding this so-called 27 club hasn't weakened the impetus for keeping their work alive, so maybe it would be good for my career if I did end up joining the club after all? And now, of course, I know that death is not something to fear, it's actually quite a beautiful experience."

"Please, Phoenix. Stop talking like this. I can't fail you."

Phoenix noticed something was underpinning Judd's words.

"Fail me? You're good at your job, Judd. The best. I couldn't ask for a better bodyguard. I must say though, that I have noticed a hint of over-protection from you. It's quite cute of you really that you care so much. I sense there's a reason you care so much though."

"I had a wife who was killed as a consequence of my actions and a girlfriend before that."

"I don't need the gory details but did you pull any metaphorical trigger yourself, Judd?"

"No."

"As I thought. So, stop beating yourself up over what it is you think you did. Life is full of ifs and buts but none of us are ever really in control, that's why the 27 club exists and that's why your wife and girlfriend died. It was not your fault. You are a good man Judd and don't ever let anyone tell you different."

"Thanks."

"Is there any other reason why you're so protective of me? It's as if you know something I don't and you're waiting for something to happen."

"Ok, perhaps I should have told you before now but I didn't want to alarm you. There was a guy over in England called Warwick Stansfield. He had articulated how he wished to do you harm. He was banged up and that took him out the equation, but then there was a RTA and he managed to escape between prisons. He is still at large and I'm worried he could be trying to track you down in order to fulfil his wishes."

"Judd, do you know how many crack-pot threats I get every day over social media or by letter even. This Stansfield guy is just one of those."

"It doesn't hurt for me to stay alert."

"Okay, I appreciate it." A short silence occurred as both Judd and Phoenix drank their tea. It was Phoenix who broke the silence. "Let's change the subject to one a little less morbid, shall we? So when our time comes to finally part company because you have protected me into my ripe old age where do you see yourself and Brooke ending up?"

"It sounds daft but I can't see me ever leaving Birmingham. I love travelling but Birmingham is always going to be my home."

"Believe me, I know what you mean. It's a great city but there may be a time when I just want to hide away somewhere remote and become a bit of a recluse with my cats."

Judd laughed. "I can't ever see you becoming a crazy cat lady."

"Stranger things have happened. I really love the South of France, Judd. You and Brooke should go there sometime. I've come to love the sun and that's something Birmingham can't offer in abundance, no matter how much like you, I love the place."

"South of France? Nice. You recorded one of your albums there didn't you?"

"Yeah, that's when I fell in love with the place. I used Studio Miraval in the Departement of the Var close to the French Riviera. I needed to be free from the press intrusion and I knew that this studio had enabled that sort of environment for George Michael to work on Wham!'s *Make It Big* album, which just happens to be one of my favourite albums. Shirley Bassey and fellow Brummies Steve Winwood and UB40 have recorded there too. How could I not be inspired to produce good music at that studio once I knew such great songs had been made there? But you see Judd, as I was saying before about an artist peaking, have I therefore already reached my peak with the music that I produced in France? I can remember feeling really inspired for that album and the music and lyrics flowed out of me with ease."

"Don't start that again. You're going to live until 105 and I'm going to be protecting you right by your side until then."

"Well, you'll have to move to the South of France with me then."

"It's a deal."

"So anyway Judd, as well as an offering of a mug of English tea I want you to have this as an appreciation of my thanks for saving my life. It's the plectrum I used on the sessions at Studio Miraval. I've had it placed on a gold chain for you. It's a special plectrum, I reckon it holds magic the way I was able to produce music with it."

Judd was gob-smacked. "Phoenix, I'm truly honoured, thank you. I don't know what to say."

"You don't have to say anything. I know you have my back and that's good enough."

"I also have your front, head, eyes, ears, boobs…"

"Err, I think we should stop right there."

The friends laughed jovially together but unfortunately, the effort of laughter resulted in Phoenix receiving a nosebleed.

Phoenix took the towel from her hair and used it to stem the flow of blood from her nose. At once Judd realised that the nosebleed was a consequence of the cocaine that Phoenix all too regularly snorted. He was just about to dis Kaleb one more time when his phone rang. It was Sab.

"Hey, Sab, what's up?"

"Oh Judd, I have some terrible news."

Judd instantly detected the distress in Sab's voice. "What is it?

"William and Crystal took their sight-seeing tour over the Grand Canyon but the small plane they were on has been reported missing. A search team are out looking for it as we speak."

Judd felt numb as he feared the worst for his friends.

CHAPTER 33
THE CONCERT AT THE GRAND CANYON

Three days had passed since Judd had received the terrible news that William and Crystal were missing. The designated search team had still not found any wreckage of the plane, but while that news served to increase anxiety levels at least it provided some hope that the popular couple could still be alive.

Judd, therefore, found himself in a distinct place of irony as he watched Phoenix bid everyone a safe journey as she closed her Grand Canyon concert. The ambitious concert performed underneath the Arizona sky had been a rip-roaring success. Not just in terms of yet another jaw-dropping musical performance by Phoenix, but also because the safety of the performer had not been compromised which of course pleased Judd. However, the feeling was one that moved to a bittersweet tone knowing that somewhere amongst the vast rocky red terrain, alive or dead, were two of his closest friends.

As the vast crowd moved away from the unprecedented event, everyone behind the scenes were 'high-fiving' one another and congratulating Phoenix on the success of the gig who had arrived dripping of sweat and sporting a beaming smile almost as wide as the Grand Canyon itself.

Judd naturally joined in with congratulating the singer and it was whilst giving Phoenix a celebratory hug (much to the irritation of Kaleb) that Judd witnessed something remarkable happen. Whilst peering over Phoenix's left shoulder as he hugged her, he was able to have a clear line of sight at the stage which was now free from the presence of any musicians. With the celebrations and high-spirits still in full flow, everyone else apart from Judd had no reason to look across at the stage. Judd couldn't believe his eyes at first. Phoenix's microphone stand rose from the floor and then levitated in mid-air, before undergoing a complete somersault and then finally crashing to its final resting place into a nearby guitar amp causing a screeching sound of feedback to resonate across the airwaves.

An unsuspecting roadie who had assumed the microphone stand had simply toppled over soon gathered the equipment and resolved the problem.

As nobody else had witnessed the flight of the microphone stand amongst the celebrations the incident wasn't given a second thought, except for Judd who reflected on the incredible sight and had taken the short amount of time to interpret the incident.

Judd understood that his friend William Chamberlain could perform acts of telekinesis and he began to sense that his friend was nearby. Judd concluded that William, whose physical abilities were already compromised even before the suspected plane crash due to his Multiple Sclerosis, had reached out to Judd by sending out a connection using the power of his mind. The signal had been strong enough to connect with the microphone stand and utilise it as an instrument to grab Judd's attention. It was the most telling sign yet that his friend was still alive.

CHAPTER 34
PHOENIX HAS LEFT THE BUILDING

The next leg of the tour saw Phoenix performing a single night on California's Venice Beach. This was a very personal and significant choice of venue for Phoenix. She loved the music of The Doors and like any fan worth their salt she realised that the beach was the very location where Jim Morrison, himself a 27-club member, and the talented keyboard player Ray Manzarek had made the fateful decision to form a band. The rest, as they say, is history.

Just like during the concert at the Grand Canyon, Brooke, Sadie and Xanthe had once again been given VIP seating in the temporary construction, whilst on this occasion, Sab in her role as a LAPD cop had joined the arrangements put in place for the security of the event. Due to the significant musical occasion, extra security resource had been required and Sab with some of her LAPD colleagues had naturally been drafted in to ably contribute. All of this assisted Judd in his quest to keep Phoenix safe from harm. And it was a good thing because Judd, much to the distress of Neima, had made the agonising decision to stay behind at the Grand Canyon and join the desperate search for William and Crystal. He had promised that he would be there for the concert and he was merely delaying his arrival, but alas with his friends still missing he had failed to get there on time, compromising his own values and desire to protect Phoenix. Judd had decided that the extra security that had been drafted in would be enough protection for the singer and although not ideal he wouldn't be missed for one concert. Concluding that William had reached out to him with the levitating microphone stand, Judd felt compelled to pursue the uncertain situation regarding his friends.

In regards to the event itself, Judd had missed a treat. Phoenix had once again provided an iconic performance on her ground-breaking and unprecedented tour.

Unfortunately, Judd had also missed something else.

Due to his absence, it had been agreed that Phoenix would leave the stage after her final encore, boycott the dressing room and backstage frivolities and instead be ushered by Kaleb of all people immediately into a waiting automobile a la Elvis style in order to swiftly drive her away to her secret hotel.

However, in spite of the swarming level of LAPD officers and concert stewards, they were oblivious to the attack on the waiting chauffeur and his subsequent gagging. The poor chap was tied up and placed into the boot of his own car.

Phoenix, of course, knew nothing of this attack on the chauffeur and as planned she successfully reached the waiting car. Once inside she turned to her boyfriend who seemed to hesitate at the car door. "Aren't you getting in Kaleb?"

"I'll follow on babe, it'll look better and confuse any paparazzi sniffing about. Don't worry this guy will look after you. He's better than that jerk, Stone, who couldn't even be bothered to be here to look after you."

Time being the essence, Phoenix saw no reason to distrust her boyfriend and relaxed further into the back seat of the car next to the seemingly hired bodyguard. It was a face she did not recognise and the bodyguard didn't greet her with as much as a 'hello'."

Once the car began to speed away from Venice Beach, the driver spoke and she recognised the voice instantly triggering her guts to churn and sending a shiver down her spine. Before she had time to fully process what was happening the man sitting next to her had placed an injection in her arm causing her to fall asleep instantly.

CHAPTER 35
THE SEARCH

"So, who are you?"

"My name is Judd Stone. I'm the best friend of William and Crystal Chamberlain, the British couple who were on the missing plane."

"So why are you here?"

"To help find my friends of course."

"Your sentiments are very noble Mr. Stone but I'm leading this very experienced rescue team so with all due respect we don't really need your help. Please, leave it to the experts."

"The same experts who haven't found anyone yet?"

"I'm not sure I like your tone Mr. Stone."

"And I am as sure as night follows day that I don't like yours, Mister?"

"My name is Ranger Lou Quaid. Listen to me. Doing a land search across this very rugged terrain in such scintillating heat is very challenging even when you do know what you're doing. You will actually weaken our cause if you choose to tag along as the chances are we will wind up compromising our time in treating you for heat exhaustion or something else. Let me assure you, we are the real experts in pursuing this quest."

"I too am such an expert?" came a voice entering the arena. Neither Judd nor Quaid had spotted the newcomer approaching them. He had long hair tied in a ponytail and his face bore the distinct features of Native American origin.

"And now who the fuck are you?" asked Quaid incredulously.

"Just another offer of help. You may not care to recognise it but my people know this land better than anyone. We have lived here for over 800 years and it is my ancestors that created the walking paths across the Canyon which you now use as hiking trails. Where is the sense in resisting an offer of help from either myself or Mr. Stone? Mr. Stone can lead us with a pure heart in an attempt to secure his friends' safety and I can assist with unrivalled knowledge of this beautiful but unforgiving land."

"I vote he stays," said Judd.

Quaid removed his sun hat which revealed a receding hairline drenched with sweat and took a couple of seconds to contemplate his next move. He looked at the other members of his search party and those who caught his eye line simply offered a shrug of the shoulders. "Ok, ok you can both tag along if it means that much to you, but let's make one thing clear. I'm in charge and I won't have me or my very experienced search team undermined."

The local man with the ponytail acknowledged with a polite nod, whereas Judd was a little less placid with his response of "whatever."

Judd instantly liked the stranger, he had a contrasting calming nature to himself but trust and confidence in him came easy. Quaid walked ahead in a strop. "Make sure you can keep up."

Ignoring Quaid, Judd shook the stranger's huge hand before they set off to join the search. "What's your name friend?"

"My name is Etu."

"Cool name."

"It means 'the sun'."

"A good name for these parts. Boy, it's hot. I'm pleased to meet you, Etu. Please call me Judd and drop this Mr. Stone nonsense."

"As you wish Judd."

They continued to walk and talk.

"Do you think you can help find my friends, Etu?"

"I believe that by working together we have a better chance."

"That's a good answer. I get the impression that your mind is more open than most?"

"My people believe that our minds must be open. There can be no alternative way of thinking. We believe in the connections we have with all that is around us: land, water and animals, so if we were to close our minds we would only be fooling and restricting ourselves."

"That makes a lot of sense. Who are your people?"

"We are the Havasupai Tribe. This means 'the people of the blue-green waters' relating to the sacred water that runs through our land and through every single member of our tribe."

"I welcome your logic and I need you to welcome mine."

"Go on."

"It's not something I cared to share with Quaid. I have a strong feeling that my friends are still alive. You see, both of my friends are able to use their mind in order to connect with people. They connect in different ways, but both can transcend the more conventional avenues of communication and the obstruction of physical matter isn't an issue."

"Then hang on to that hope Judd. Without hope, we will never find them."

The night was drawing in and it was agreed that the land search should retire for the night. A temporary camp was set up so that the team could rest and recharge their metaphorical batteries. The aerial search being conducted by others had unfortunately also produced nothing of note.

Judd and Etu naturally migrated to one another and they settled down to eat their evening meal. It had been Etu who had created the campfire.

"I'm not too keen on this survival food," joked Judd. "In any case, I'm not hungry."

"You must eat, Judd. Stay strong for your friends…Even if it does taste like shit."

Judd couldn't help but laugh in spite of the increasing desperate situation. "Do you still have hope of finding them Etu?"

"Have you received any messages or signs today?"

"No, I have not. That's why I'm worried."

"I have."

"Really?" asked Judd widening his eyes with anticipation.

"Yes, sir. Earlier today I noticed that we crossed the tracks of the opossum along the dusty ground. Crossing the tracks of animals have significant meaning to the people of Havasupai. The opossum is an animal of underestimated intellect. It possesses the ability to free itself from the most challenging situations no matter how powerful it's enemy. It uses its mind rather than its brawn. Remind you of anyone? The opossum may even resort to playing dead if it has too. In particular, could your friend William be like the opossum? No doubt your friend is cunning and clever and able to use his mind when called upon but for now, believes there is a need to relax the powers of his mind. Performing acts of telekinesis, I'm sure can be very draining on any physical residual energy. Perhaps he has sensed that you are seeking him and that's enough? Or perhaps he too is needing to play dead for some reason?"

"I'd like to think that was possible, Etu. But if he could send me a signal of some kind that would help matters, surely he'd know that?"

"Look around you, Judd. Ok, now it's dark, but you've seen the vastness of this landscape, you may be closer than you think and he may also know that, so why send out a signal that could perhaps confuse the energies of the pursuit?"

"You're not just a pretty face are you, Etu?"

"Did you notice any other animal tracks today, Judd?"

"Can't say I was looking, mate. To tell you the truth I wouldn't know the difference between a coyote or a large rabbit anyhow."

"I saw the tracks of a muskrat. The sighting of this animal's footprints especially gave me hope."

"Go on."

"The muskrat represents resilience and the ability to adapt to its surroundings in order to survive. I believe that the tracks I saw means that the muskrat is representing the resilience and adaptability of your friends, including if it is either land or water that is involved with their current situation, and it gives us the strength to adapt to our journey in finding your friends. Importantly it signifies that a positive outcome is probable even in the bleakest of circumstances."

"That's really heartening stuff, Etu. Thank you. I'd never have known such things and to think that the friendly Ranger Quaid didn't want you to come along."

"Ranger Quaid has his methods and I don't doubt his intentions but the more hands that push against the crumbling wall the better chance we have of keeping it standing." Etu then placed down the metal dish he was eating from and grasped a handful of earth. He looked straight at Judd. "Your friendship with William and Crystal is a good one, Judd and the love in your heart cannot go unrewarded. This here earth has been kind to my people for generations upon generations. Hold on to what is good in life, Judd even if it's a handful of earth."

"Etu, you and your people have a clear connection with what the elements of our planet can teach us. It's truly impressive. But tell me, do numbers hold any power or knowledge for you or your people?"

"Why do you ask, Judd?"

"Have you ever heard of the pop star Phoenix?"

"Of course, I have, Judd. Who hasn't? We don't all live in wigwams in the middle of nowhere these days. I've even been known to watch television from time to time."

"Sorry, that was pretty dumb of me."

Etu smiled. "No problem, my friend. So, you were going to tell me about numbers."

"I want to talk to you about numerology."

"Ok."

"The reason I'm over here is to protect Phoenix, I'm her bodyguard."

"Really? That's some responsibility, Judd. Is Phoenix in any kind of specific danger?" (With no mobile phone signal in the heart of the Grand Canyon, word had not yet reached Judd of Phoenix's dilemma.)

"Well, I need to prevent her from joining the 27 club?"

"The 27 club?"

"The name given to a bunch of superstars who died at the untimely age of 27: Jim Morrison, Jimi Hendrix, Janis Joplin, Kurt Cobain, Amy Winehouse, they are all so-called members of this cursed club and there are more besides."

"Why would the number 27 be so prevalent?"

"I maybe hoped you could enlighten me with a whole different angle on it?"

Etu searched his mind. "Not really, Judd. The number four is the number that interests us."

"Number four? It doesn't divide or anything into 27 as far as I know. Maths was never my strongest subject at school."

"The number four has key symbolism for us. There are

four winds for example."

"Back to the connection with nature again."

"Yes. But sorry I can't offer anything to help you with the number 27. Is Phoenix really in danger do you think?"

"It's possible but not as much as my friends William and Crystal are right now."

If only Judd knew the reality of Phoenix's situation.

The search started again bright and early the next morning. The temporary camp was expertly dismantled and packed away for use at another time.

Three hours into the trek Judd received his strongest inspiration yet. The search team came to a point in the trail which presented a fork which led to two different pathways. Quaid was about to lead them to the pathway on the right when Judd felt an overwhelming sense to veer to the left. He shared his thoughts with Quaid but typically Quaid wasn't convinced.

"What do you mean you've got a feeling?" asked Quaid, Judd felt that he was almost mocking him. "We can't focus the search on the basis that someone has a feeling in their gut."

"It's more than that, it's a very strong pull. It's actually making me feel quite nauseous."

"That could just be the climate. It's tough out here, we can give you more water if you need it and we can rest for a while. Hell, we could all do with a rest anyhow."

"I know it sounds crazy, but I can sense a bright light guiding me to distinctly continue our journey on the pathway on the left."

"That bright light, it's just the sun, Judd."

"Really? So, where's the sun right now, Quaid?"

Quaid took a moment to briefly scan the sky before answering. "East, I guess."

"East, and I want to go left which is bound for the west. Listen, Quaid, I'm going with you or without you but I know for sure that my friends are over that way." Judd pointed along the left-sided pathway with his index finger.

Etu spoke next. "Ranger, we have enough supplies and bodies to split the journey. If we could take two or three of your expert team to travel west the rest of you can travel to the east."

Quaid thought over the proposition.

"I don't know. You're all in my care and in spite of what you may think of me your safety is of the most paramount importance to me."

"And finding my friends is of the most paramount importance to me," said Judd. The feeling to head along the left-sided fork was compelling, almost like a magnetic force sucking his whole being and spirit towards that direction. He was convinced that the strong feelings that he was experiencing had to be some kind of mind projection coming from William.

"Very well," Quaid looked to his experienced team and offered three people: two women and one man. "Keri, Laverne and Davey. You are three of my most experienced team, you break off with Stone and the Indian."

"The Indian has a name," snapped Judd.

Quaid became sarcastic, the heat adding to his impatience. "Forgive me, I've forgotten it that's all. Remind me of the name again."

"Etu," replied Etu himself.

"Right, do it now team before I change my mind. Give Etu and Judd a helping hand down the other trail. I guess by splitting up it means we get two bites at the cherry."

"Thank you," said Judd, genuinely.

Quaid also began to mellow. "You're welcome. Good luck. When all this is over the members of the team will get you back safely."

There were shaking of hands, hugs and motivational smacks on backs before the two parties went their separate ways.

After a few minutes, Etu shared another one of his stories with Judd. "Judd to split up is not a bad thing and I believe that your hunch is right."

"Can you feel what I feel too?"

"No, I'm afraid I can't. That is your friend connecting with you but what I can tell you is that we are heading towards the protection of the Wigleeva. I believe the Wigleeva is standing guard over your friends, keeping them safe until you find them and bring them home."

"What is the Wigleeva?"

"They are two huge red pillars of rock that we believe guard the Havasupai tribe. As I told you before, we are at one with nature and therefore that includes this rugged land. You see Judd, we are also heading towards the two rock formations that form the image of a man and a woman holding a child. I believe that the warmth of the family image is drawing you to your family of William and Crystal. Once, many years ago, the Havasupai tribe also decided to split in order to find new resources as the resources reduced in line with the tribe's population increasing over time. A man, woman and child made the decision to turn back, too distraught to leave the area which they loved and knew and because of that fateful decision they were turned to stone. It is fitting that a man called Stone is now leading us that way with his heart.

As it turned out Judd's decision to follow his heart whilst being pulled by an indescribable magnetic force to head west had been sound, and his decision before that to stay behind from travelling onward with Phoenix's tour hadn't been fully ill-advised either. It had been he who had been able to lead the rescue team through nothing more than the unexplained power of strong signals that were entering his mind. Judd knew this must have been William guiding him, or perhaps even Crystal who was well in tune with other-worldly things - or perhaps both!

The rescue team had been in a desperate state after so many days of not finding the plane wreckage that Quaid had been willing to split the party once the option had been presented to him. Allowing some of his team to go with Judd's conviction resulted in the wreckage being found under the scorching sun. Judd had been correct in taking the path west.

What Judd and the team discovered was truly harrowing. The bulk of the small plane had remained partially intact but fragments of metal were scattered amongst the crash scene, blistered seats were now positioned independent to the aircraft and a series of blood-soaked deceased or badly injured bodies were lying in and amongst the wreckage.

Sadly, the pilot hadn't made it but William and Crystal were part of the small number who had been found alive, which presented something of a miracle considering the impact of the crash coupled with the harsh heat. They were dehydrated and heavily sunburnt with some very painful injuries, but thankfully none were life-changing. Above all, they had each been found with a strong pulse in spite of their state of unconsciousness. The main race against time would be to get William's Multiple Sclerosis medication into his system. Judd had had the presence of mind to have brought some with him.

"I'm here buddy, I've got you," said Judd taking hold of his friend's hand.

William acknowledged the presence of his rescuer by giving a weak squeeze. It was enough for Judd to know he had his friend back. He glanced over at Crystal and admired Keri's attentiveness as she expertly nursed his other friend. One of the initial actions was to simply pour water into Crystal's dry mouth.

So, after finding his friends alive the feeling of relief for Judd became immeasurable, however not long after the feeling turned to despair once he learned of Phoenix's suspected kidnap when the cell phone signals eventually kicked in.

CHAPTER 36
DEATH OF A PRIVATE INVESTIGATOR

"Thank you for identifying the body, Miss Mistry," said the detective.

"Ted had no other family. I'm not family either but we had become close friends. He didn't deserve this."

"I'm sorry for your loss."

As tough a cookie Yasmin was, having to identify a dead body at her tender age was very hard to do. She distinctively felt a chill in the air. The sterile environment which surrounded her with the most neutral decoration imaginable did little to ease her sorrow.

"How did he die?"

"We believe he took his own life."

"Poor Ted. He had suffered years of depression, but I really thought he was ok recently."

"Sadly, that can often happen. When someone makes the decision to end their life their mood visibly seems to lift as they come to terms with what they believe they need to do in order to end their pain."

"So, what happened. Did he leave a note?"

"Not that we know of."

"So how do you know it was suicide?" typically Yasmin didn't hold back on the direct delivery of her words.

"He was stood amongst a crowd of people who had gathered at a busy road crossing and witnesses said all of a sudden he seemed to just throw himself under a lorry"

"He could have been pushed."

"I understand that this kind of thing can be hard to accept Miss Mistry but there were no witness statements to suggest that was the case."

"They may not have seen it happen…if it was done properly."

"Miss Mistry, I can assure you, we have no reason to suspect foul play."

Yasmin wasn't convinced. She felt numb. "He was a private detective. He made enemies."

"Anyone in particular?"

"If I said yes would you follow it up?" The silence answered Yasmin's question.

"As I thought. No, no one in particular."

CHAPTER 37
THE HOSTAGE

The Saturn Rising Motel had been uninhabited for the best part of two decades and was an ideal location to harbour a victim of a kidnapping. The apparent abandonment by the motel's proprietors remained a mystery, not that it mattered much to the kidnappers. The motel, except for the odd broken window, seemed to have been left untouched with its entire stock of furniture, bedding and room keys all at the ready. This gave an eerie atmosphere to the isolated establishment and its remote location was most likely the reason for any commercial decline and lack of interest since its abandonment.

The climate was nearly always dry and dusty at the motel but this had still not prevented rambling pockets of overgrown foliage to take hold, including at times through the internal floorboards of the rooms.

Phoenix Easter was being held captive in room nine. Her kidnappers had chained both her arms to the headboard of the bed and had her gagged for most of the time, usually only removing the cloth to allow her to eat and drink. It was despicable to think that the most listened to singing voice of its generation was being silenced this way.

Ziggy pulled a dining chair up to the bedside, then pulled a large knife with a jagged blade from his pocket and grinned as he teased it along Phoenix's body. Phoenix flinched as the blade first stroked against her thighs and then Ziggy circled it across her stomach and breasts before applying the pressure of the blade a little more when he reached her cheek causing a small droplet of blood to appear. Phoenix became really scared when the blade hovered above her eye, but then Ziggy sat back in the chair and pulled the knife away leaving Phoenix only slightly relieved but still guessing her fate. He kept the knife in his hands and firmly in full view as he spoke.

"You can see that I wouldn't hesitate to carve you up in an instant little girl if I don't get my money. You see, Phoenix, you owe me. You fired me in a heartbeat and that was after all I'd done for you. You were happy to have me around when you wanted something to lift your mood were you not? All those times I put my neck on the line to get you the highs you wanted, and then what do you go and do? You get rid of me. Just like that. You didn't show me the slightest amount of respect or loyalty. Not like my cousin, he's very loyal to me as it happens. Did you notice how Kaleb didn't exactly bust a gut to help you out?"

Phoenix squeezed her eyes shut at the realisation that Kaleb knew this was going to happen and had done nothing to stop it. He had clearly been an integral part of the whole kidnapping plot. How could he betray her like that?

Ziggy continued with his warped rant. "Do you know what really pissed my cousin off? You replaced me with that chump, Stone. It didn't please me too much either. Well, it's payback time, one way or another if you catch my drift. So, you'd better hope that the same chump brings me the money I'm owed. Let's call it a compensation payment. Of course, I'll see my cousin right too. Financially I mean, he deserves it after all the shit he's had to put up with being chained to you."

"Don't forget that's a compensation payment for both of us, Ziggy. I'm owed to."

The voice came from the other kidnapper who up until this point hadn't spoken too often. The same guy who had stuck a needle in her arm sending her to sleep whilst sitting next to her in the back of the car. He walked out of the bathroom and disturbingly remained standing close to the bed. His stare went right through Phoenix and he gave her the creeps.

"Don't worry Mr. Stansfield, I haven't forgotten that you're owed something too. Phoenix, I don't believe you've been properly introduced to Mr. Stansfield. He's a very well-educated man and from the most finest English breeding so it's been an enormous pleasure to do business with him. The thing is, which isn't such great news for you, is that Mr. Stansfield is also a very dangerous man. He's currently a fugitive, you know. You're very fortunate, he wanted to kill you and Mr. Stone, but I convinced him that before we do any such thing we should secure a financial reward for ourselves."

Ziggy began to use the point of the knife's blade to clean the dirt from under his fingernails as if to underline his total control on things. He continued to speak at Phoenix.

"Stone fancies himself as a bit of a hero so I knew the best way to get to him was through you. He won't be able to resist being the knight in shining armour turning up to rescue his damsel in distress, but when he shows with our money - 'bang' - your good Samaritan will meet his maker, and nothing will bring me more pleasure than to see his arrogant ass hit the floor like a wrecking ball. He took my job and he took my credibility when he attacked me and he's going to pay for taking such fucking liberties.

"Then, personally, once I have your money and Stone is no more I'd be happy to let you go, but unfortunately I think Mr. Stansfield has other ideas for you Phoenix. You see, he believes that it is his personal duty to fulfil the prophecy of the 27 club. He is very influential too you know, being such a well-educated man and all, he really knows how to pitch his beliefs. I'll have to see how I feel at the time about trying to persuade him that you should live, Phoenix, but one thing's for sure: if Stone doesn't bring us our money you will die.

"So, I'm sure that you can see how we are going to need the money in order to start new lives? Neither of us wants to hang around and do time for ridding the world of a lowlife such as Judd Stone. And imagine if we are responsible for the death of a much-loved superstar too!"

Unable to speak or move effectively, Phoenix squeezed her eyes shut after catching sight of Stansfield smirking at that last remark. Closing her eyes seemed her only viable option to react somehow.

"Anyway, it's been nice talking to you, Phoenix. It's time to give our Mr. Stone a call and provide him with some very explicit instructions."

CHAPTER 38
THE DROP

Wisely or unwisely Judd had obeyed his instruction not to involve the police. He hadn't even told Sab that he had been contacted and the police in America currently believed that they were simply dealing with a missing person situation, albeit a very well-known missing person. They kept an open mind but the overriding assumption was that the unconventional and self-destructive Phoenix Easter had merely decided to go AWOL for reasons that only she would understand why.

Kaleb had also done his best to send the trail cold by informing anyone who would listen that Phoenix had hinted that she needed time to recharge her batteries. Apparently, she had confided in him that a tour of this unprecedented nature was both physically and mentally demanding on her. Judd had never believed the snake's story even before he had received the call from Ziggy, which of course fully clarified the precarious position for both him and Phoenix.

Although he had chosen not to involve the police, Judd had decided that he needed to inform Neima otherwise there would be no hope of being able to raise the amount of cash that was being demanded. Neima had wanted to accompany him to the abandoned motel for obvious reasons but he had managed to convince her that it was too dangerous and that he was on top of the situation due to his previous career experiences. He had also managed to convince Neima not to mention anything to Brooke. He figured that the fewer people knew the more he was in control of being able to rescue Phoenix, even if that meant harbouring a secret from his wife of only a few days.

The drive to the desolated motel had been a long one, but eventually, Judd pulled into the sun-soaked car park and a cloud of dust surrounded the wheels as he braked to a halt. When he stepped out of the car into the lingering dust clouds, clutching a holdall full of money, Ziggy was already waiting for him with his eye firmly staring down the barrel of a rifle which was pointing straight at Judd.

"I trust that holdall's full of money," said the criminal.

"Of course."

"For once it looks like you haven't let your ego overrule your head, Stone. No police I see. Or perhaps it's to the contrary, your ego may have convinced you that you can become Phoenix's knight in shining armour. Well, think again."

"I gave you my word, now you keep yours and hand Phoenix over to me."

"Once I have the money."

"Why don't you come and get it?"

"Because last time we danced I came away the loser."

"Ziggy, you're pointing a gun right down my throat. I'm not even armed. Come on over and I'll hand it to you."

"Like I fully trust you, Stone. Now open the holdall and show me what's inside. For all I know there's fuck all in it."

"Judd unzipped the holdall, pulled the opening wide and held the bag out to Ziggy so that he could see the stash of bank notes."

"Ok, now really slowly I want you to throw the money as far as you can towards me and then place your hands in the air. If you try anything funny I'll blow your fucking brains out and the world will never see Phoenix Easter again."

Judd complied with Ziggy's instructions. He threw the bag towards Ziggy who kept his eyes on Judd as he scurried towards the holdall and retrieved it, retreating as quickly as he could with the gun continually pointing at Judd.

"Now, Ziggy. You have what you want, release the girl."

"I don't think you are in any position to call the shots, Stone. You'll see her soon enough, but first, there's someone else who's just dying to meet you."

When no-one appeared, Ziggy shouted louder. "I said, there's someone here just dying to meet you?" Ziggy had shouted loud enough to send some turkey vultures flying into the blue sky who had been picking at an unrecognisable animal carcass nearby.

Judd kept his hands in the air but shrugged his shoulders.

"Stansfield, get your ass out here and leave that pretty wench tied up a second."

Ziggy now had Judd's full attention on hearing the name. "Stansfield! Warwick Stansfield? You left Phoenix alone with that psycho you fucking moron."

"Do you want a bullet in your skull, Stone? You'd better watch your mouth."

"He's probably slicing and dicing her right now as we speak you stupid fat fuck. Listen, stop fucking about. You have to let me into her, Ziggy."

Ziggy appeared anxious, he had actually intended to keep his part of the deal once he had the dough and let Phoenix go. Now it came to it he was even rethinking if the 'torture time' he originally had planned for Judd should materialize. He knew Stansfield was a psycho and he no longer felt in control. For a split second he looked over towards room nine and it was just enough time for Judd to pull out a pistol which he had sneakily tucked down the back of his jeans. This now created a standoff between Judd and Ziggy as each had a firearm pointing at the other.

"You sly fuck, Stone. I knew you couldn't be trusted."

"You should have grown a pair and searched me you twat. Now if you fancy your chances go ahead but I'm telling you now, I'm going to go over to that room over there and I'm going to attend to Phoenix and you had better pray that I'm not too late."

Suddenly a car appeared from nowhere tearing up the dusty road.

"I told you no fucking pol-" but before Ziggy could complete his sentence a bullet entered his head and he dropped to the floor. Judd checked his gun not quite believing what was happening and he confirmed to himself that not a single bullet had been fired from his gun.

The car continued on its journey and headed straight for the motel. Two shots were fired from its windows blowing out the front tyres on Judd's car before it effortlessly crashed through the wall of room nine. Judd watched two men get out of the car, one who was huge in size and noticed the other one of them curiously holding a black umbrella in spite of the scorching heat. Judd recognised who it was immediately.

Ray Talia ran back out of the motel followed by the biggest guy Judd had ever seen. This second guy had Phoenix Easter draped over his shoulder. She raised her head and made eye contact with Judd. She was alive but clearly injured because it was her blood which was increasingly staining the large man's white T-shirt.

Ray opened one of the rear doors of the car and in spite of the speed of the operation, the large man lay Phoenix on the back seat with a great deal of care where another unknown man was waiting who immediately began to nurse her wounds. The beast of a man then jumped in the front of the car himself. Ray was content to jump in the boot and sit there facing outwards leaving the metal lid aloft.

As the car sped away the driver's window came down and Judd saw the gorgeous face of Gia Talia appear and blow him a kiss. Within an instant the car was heading off away from the motel and Ray wearing his best crazy smile waved a sardonic goodbye to Judd until the car became a dot on the dusty horizon.

It had all happened so fast Judd had been taken totally by surprise and was at a loss as to how he should react. Ziggy was dead, that was good, but should he have fired at Ray and his sidekick? He had a gun, why not? But it seemed clear that they were on Phoenix's side and taking a shot at the notorious Talia was never a healthy move for anyone. Not even Judd.

Judd ran towards room nine and entered cautiously holding his gun out in front of him. The room had been trashed following the car smash but he could clearly see a dead Warwick Stansfield lying on the bed with a bullet wound in his forehead and a black umbrella sticking from his eye.

At least he still had all that money to take home with him but agonisingly he didn't have Phoenix. He was her damn bodyguard for Christ' sake and despite everything he had gone through today she was still not in his care.

Then it dawned on him that his long return journey ahead was going to have to be done in a car with no front tyres!

But then a stroke of luck appeared. As he left the demolished room he saw a car parked opposite. He walked over towards it and was delighted to discover that it was unlocked with the keys sitting in the ignition. Perhaps there was a god after all, he thought. All he needed to do was collect the money and head back but he knew that he wouldn't be able to catch up with Gia and Ray.

As he stepped into the car he heard a banging that seemed to be coming from the boot. He walked to the rear of the car and reached for the button causing the lid of the boot to swing open. The smell on opening nearly floored him. Judd discovered the original chauffeur who had been hired to drive Phoenix away from Venice Beach, gagged and tied and unfortunately covered in his own urine and soiling.

Judd took a step back and hoped that the deserted motel still had running water before he had to share a car with this dude.

CHAPTER 39
THE LATEST MEMBER

"What do you mean she's dead?" screamed Neima.

"I'm truly sorry to have to tell you this, Neima. I know how fond you were of Phoenix. We all were." Gia Talia seemed as sincere as Judd had ever seen her but he still wasn't convinced.

"When I saw that lump carry Phoenix out of that wrecked motel room she was very much alive."

"It wasn't the injuries that killed her Judd. Well not directly anyway. Phoenix suffered a cardiac arrest, most likely brought on by the shock and trauma of her ordeal coupled with the weak state of her heart caused by her excessive drugs and alcohol abuse."

"Bullshit," shouted Judd. "She was in great physical condition. There's no way she could have performed those last two shows if she had a dodgy ticker."

"Sadly, the strain of those performances probably also contributed to her heart giving way. At least she went out at the top of her game," said Gia.

Neima sat down on the sofa and placed her head between her hands. "I can't believe she's dead. I won't believe it."

"I have the death certificate here," said Gia handing the document to Neima. "It's signed by a doctor and the coroner is content that a post-mortem was not necessary indicating that Phoenix didn't suffer a violent and unnatural death. It was a heart attack that took her from us and therefore natural causes."

"Natural causes? She was 27 years old," Judd was livid.

"It's there in black and white, Judd," said Gia with a sterner tone in her voice.

"How much did you pay to ensure that piece of paper said what you wanted it to? I know you, Gia Talia, you have the ability to pay almost anyone off, or even persuade them to see your way of thinking if necessary. Did you set your hired monkeys loose?"

This time Gia raised her voice. "You're not thinking this through, Judd."

"That's exactly what I am doing."

"Oh, really. So why did we rescue her from the clutches of those two pieces of filth Stansfield and Ziggy then? We went to all that trouble to rescue her simply because we wanted to do the job ourselves, did we? I don't think so. We tried to rescue her and because we succeeded she was at least able to pass away peacefully in the company of people who cared for her. A bit more gratitude wouldn't be out of place, Stone."

"We cared about her. We should have been with her when she died," sobbed Neima.

Gia calmed herself in order to comfort Neima. "I'm sorry, Neima. If it had have been possible you would have been with her for her last moments. But then again, she would never have wanted you to be burdened with this side of things. She cared about you too."

"Phoenix could never have been a burden," wept Neima.

"Phoenix was the most exquisite success story to have ever come out of Birmingham and we were always around in the background keeping an eye out for our prize asset. You know that in spite of her flawed lifestyle, which we all struggled to witness, Phoenix was smart beyond her years and so it made sense to her to hire us to take care of the legal side of things on her behalf. She was a proud Brummie and she wanted to utilise Birmingham's most lucrative business associates."

"Business associates? Don't make me laugh. You're a bunch of fucking gangsters."

Gia was becoming increasingly irritated with Judd. "Look, I know you're upset Judd, but if you keep up with this line of disrespectfulness you're going to find out just what type of gangsters we are." Gia turned her attention back to Neima. "We looked after all of Phoenix's legal matters including her last will and testament. Didn't you ever wonder Neima why you were kept apart from that side of things? Phoenix knew all that morbid stuff would upset you so she left you to do what you were good at and left us to do what we were good at."

"So where is she now, Gia? Where's Phoenix's body?" asked Judd.

"Phoenix was always keen to have a quick cremation when the time came. She liked the Irish tradition of how they conducted their funerals within a couple of days, but she didn't extend to wanting the wake to go with it. She wanted a small, quiet and private cremation which wouldn't be turned into a circus by the media. As you know, Phoenix was a very selfless person, so you may find it strange that the likes of you were not invited but she didn't want anyone dwelling on her death or getting upset at her funeral. Instead, remember her how you knew her. That's what she wanted."

Just then a knock came at the door. Gia took the lead to open it and allowed her brother into the room. "This is for you Ms. Sage."

Ray handed Neima a black marble urn with a guitar-shaped plaque upon it made from pure gold. Inscribed on the guitar was a single word. Phoenix.

"Thank you," said Neima accepting the urn.

Ray removed his trilby hat as a mark of respect. "I'm truly sorry for your loss, Ms. Sage."

"If only I could somehow make this Phoenix rise from her ashes." Neima managed a smile.

Judd still wasn't necessarily buying all of this but he resisted from stating that the ashes in the urn could have easily been that of anything, or anyone and not necessarily those of Phoenix. He knew more than anyone just what the Talias were capable of. But he could also see the way Neima was hugging the urn close to her chest and how extensive she was sobbing as she rocked back and forth. He didn't have the heart to challenge the situation any further at this moment in time. Besides, he had to concede that Gia had seemed genuine enough. Who was he to doubt proceedings?

"You may want to keep the ashes, Neima, or perhaps scatter them somewhere that Phoenix was fond of."

"For now, Gia, they'll be coming home with me to Birmingham. I'll decide from there what to do with them. Phoenix at least deserves to be taken back to the city she loved."

"That's a good idea. Birmingham is somewhere we all need to head home to now. There's no point hanging around in the US any longer."

"So, there'll be no grave for fans to pay their respects," asked Judd, a little calmer now.

"That's what Phoenix wanted, Judd. She didn't want any platform whatsoever where the media could benefit from her death."

"Except she has joined the 27 club now. Something I hoped would never happen. They'll be writing about that sure enough."

"I dare say they will, but Phoenix can only control what's in her gift."

"Can?" enquired Judd.

"Sorry, could. I keep speaking about her in the present tense. It's hard to accept that Phoenix has gone, it's like she's still here."

"Isn't it just," said Judd.

"When we are back in Birmingham we can go over the will in a bit more detail. It's not important now. However, I can tell you now Neima that Phoenix has left you her entire Warwickshire estate."

"That's sweet of her, though I'd swap it all to have her back for just one more day."

"We will take over ownership and the running of Phoenix's club 'The Edge of Heaven'."

"I'm surprised that you're not going to rename it 'Club 27'," Judd couldn't help himself. He still felt a sense of cynicism somewhere with all of this.

"We are going to rename the club actually. It will simply be called 'Heaven' as Phoenix has now stepped over the edge so to speak."

Judd resisted informing the room that Phoenix wasn't even a believer.

"Judd, your services were recognised by Phoenix too, albeit you weren't together for a lengthy amount of time. I do know she liked you a lot. I believe she had already given you a guitar plectrum on a chain when she was alive. Well, now you've got the guitar to go with it. Phoenix has willed you her black Rickenbacker 325 guitar. John Lennon had one just like it and she knows, err knew, that you are a big fan of the Beatle."

Judd's eyes filled up. "Wow, that's truly amazing. I'm very grateful to her. I always will be for the short time I had the privilege of being her bodyguard."

"The guitar is in safekeeping. You will have it soon, Judd."

"Thank you."

"We are going to refurbish the club so that it will become a fitting memorial to Phoenix, you know install some over-sized images of Phoenix for example and some wall art that represents her work."

"This is all moving too fast, for me," said Neima.

"I'm sorry, said Gia. "Let's leave it there and perhaps we can all have a chat back in Birmingham. I'm sorry once again to be the bearer of this sad news."

Sad but very convenient news thought Judd. Everything seemed very much in its place for someone who had unexpectedly died at the untimely age of 27. But then again perhaps Phoenix had planned things meticulously well in advance of her death, after all, she had discussed the possibility of her dying young with him before.

"Watch how you go Gia, Ray," offered Judd.

"Thanks, Judd. You too. You're looking good considering the circumstances," smiled Gia warmly.

"You too."

"Oh Ray, before you go what's this thing you're doing all about? Why are you suddenly carrying a black umbrella everywhere you go?"

Gia answered for him. "My baby brother fancies himself as a bit of a Mr. Bond these days."

Then Ray spoke for himself. "An umbrella is a very easy thing to carry around with you and much less conspicuous than a gun, but when the tip is laced with poison it's just as effective a weapon. My only regret is that Warwick Stansfield was dead before I'd had the pleasure of seeing him squirm from the poison that entered his eye. The laced umbrella will be my weapon of choice forever going forward."

Judd refrained from informing Ray that he was just a gangster rather than some kind of special agent. It was no surprise that Ray had such illusions of grandeur, Judd had noticed the signs before when he had worked for him as a debt collector. The guy was dangerously unhinged to say the least. However, although it was an extreme approach and Ray was clearly playing out a fantasy, Judd was actually taken with the idea of using an umbrella in such a way –

and if it assisted in the killing of Warwick Stansfield who was he to criticize?

Once Gia and Ray had left, Judd sat down next to Neima and willingly took the sobbing lady into his arms.

As he comforted Neima and glanced down at the black marble urn that held Phoenix's ashes something painful crossed his mind. What song had she dedicated to him on the day she performed on the rooftop of the Rotunda Building? "Don't Let Me Down." Well, now he could add Phoenix Easter to the increasing list of women whom he believed he had failed to prevent from coming to harm.

CHAPTER 40
THE SURPRISE

Kaleb turned off the bath taps in order to stem the flow of water and slipped his scrawny frame into the welcoming steamy pool. He had trailed an electrical extension lead from the plug socket positioned in the hallway so that he could power the mini hi-fi that he had just about managed to balance on the window ledge. The window ledge sat directly above the bath. He gave an ironic smile as his favourite track of Phoenix's blasted out from the speakers just as he further immersed his body into the water. He continued to smile as he closed his eyes and allowed the relaxing water to engulf his flat chest and narrow shoulders. The radio stations were playing her songs more than ever lately since the announcement of her untimely death. But pretty soon his smile faded when he thought about his dead cousin and the fact that he hadn't seen a penny of the money he had been expecting from the botched kidnap plot.

And there had been nothing put aside for him in Phoenix's will either.

He closed his eyes once more, relaxed and injected a

pre-prepared syringe in an arm which was already peppered with needle marks. The injected heroin, coupled with the sensation of water, began to drift Kaleb down an imaginary stream from all the confusion and bitterness that he was feeling. The rhythmic sound of the music also began to conspire with the drug to allow Kaleb to enter into a state of sheer bliss.

However, he was just about alert enough to open his eyes when he heard a familiar voice at the foot of his bath.

"Hello Kaleb."

The water splashed like a mini-tsunami as the startled Kaleb bolted upright in the tub.

"What's the matter, Kaleb? You look like you've seen a ghost."

Kaleb rubbed his eyes as if that would somehow make who he was looking at disappear. "You're not real. I'm hallucinating, that's all. It's the heroin making me see things that aren't really there. You're not real. You can't be."

They were the last words Kaleb Rodriguez ever spoke as the hi-fi found its way into the bath water causing the junkie to sizzle, fry and jump like an electrically-charged catfish on a pole.

The miserable life of Kaleb Rodriquez was over at the age of 27.

CHAPTER 41
THE BLOOD SACRIFICE THAT NEARLY WAS

Judd Stone found himself in familiar territory as he sat opposite Ocran Le Boeuf with his eyes icily fixed on him. Ocran just happened to be tied to a chair just like many other unwise men before him who had been foolish enough to cross Judd Stone.

"We underestimated you, didn't we Ocran?"

"What the hell are you talking about?"

"Hell. A very opportune word. We'll come back to that. The thing is Ocran, you underestimated me too. That was your mistake. Before I was a bodyguard to the rich and famous I was a cop so I know how to sniff out pieces of shit like you."

"So, tell me. What's this all about?"

"It's about you wanting to offer Phoenix Easter up for a blood sacrifice."

Ocran forced a false laugh. "A blood sacrifice? Are you nuts? You truly are insane aren't you, Stone?"

"You're the fucking nutter mate. You and your fucking narcissistic mates."

"My mates?"

"Yeah, that's right. Now I don't know if you are actually the bonafide Illuminati or some other secret society like what I see splattered all over social media and what I read about in countless conspiracy theories, but I do know that you belong to a group of people that want to control everyone and everything."

Le Boeuf was scared by now, it seemed he had indeed underestimated the dangerous man sitting before him, but still, he tried to exude an air of bravado. "Really?"

"Yeah, really."

"And who else is in this imaginary group then, Stone?"

"Some very powerful people. I'm under no illusion, Ocran. There are people from the media, politics, the church and even the law. Oh, and sometimes the odd dickhead from a fucking record company."

"Ok, ok. Very clever Sherlock. But you will know that these people you speak of won't take kindly to you fucking with one of their own."

This time Judd laughed. "I don't care about you and your warped cronies, Le Boeuf. You see, due to my career experience and previous profession I also know how to cover my tracks. No one knows you're here and no one will ever find your body."

Le Boeuf visibly gulped. "My body? Now come on Stone, this has gone far enough. Let me go and we'll say no more about it."

"Mmmm, sorry mate no can do. You didn't show poor old Ted any mercy when you discovered he was on to you, did you? I know you pushed him under that lorry you evil bastard."

"You can't prove that."

"I don't have to. But you should think yourself very lucky that it's me sorting you out and not Ted's friend Yasmin who was particularly pissed at what you did to her friend. Yasmin would have given you an even slower and painful death than I'm about to. Anyway, not only will I avenge Ted, I also owe it to Phoenix to punish you appropriately. You see, I know that you had planned to kill her. Ted knew it too and that's why you silenced him."

"Why on earth would I want to kill Phoenix? She was my biggest selling artist."

"Exactly, and as you have found out since her death her records have sold as many again. And now documentaries are being released, there's talks of a biopic film, books are being written - all of which help to line your pocket. You wanted her dead alright but somebody beat you to the punch."

"You have it all worked out don't you, Stone. There's no flies on you I'll give you that much. She'd reached her peak. She wasn't going to top that unique tour that she'd come up with or that last album of hers."

Suddenly Judd's anger spiked which didn't go unnoticed on Le Boeuf. "For my money, Phoenix still had lots of excellent music to offer. Sadly, we'll never know. I reckon that you'd have let her do a few more of those high-profile venues on the tour before striking though. There were still a few more money earners to be had before the time was right to hand her over to your so-called Master."

"You dare to mock Satan? If you've done your research half as well as you claim you have Stone, you're being extremely foolish."

Judd was impassive. "It wasn't Phoenix who needed to offer herself up as a blood sacrifice in exchange for her fame and fortune, it was you and your sick gang of weirdos who were going to do it on her behalf because you believed that she had almost reached the point where she was worth more to you dead than alive. And tying it all in with the 27 Club membership wouldn't have done any harm either, would it? It really annoys me Le Boeuf that the poor girl didn't have a clue what macabre plan was being plotted behind her back and that's still after all the millions of pounds that she had already made for you, you greedy bastard. Let me picture the scene for you. You were going to lay the poor cow out while some sacrificial drums banged all around her whilst you and your freaks performed some crazy ritual dressed in cloaks and masks before finally driving some sort of prestigious blade into that beautiful body of hers. Am I warm?"

"They will find you, Stone. You're making a big mistake."

"Mistake or not I am going to kill you. You wanted Phoenix to join the 27 club and that I'm afraid just won't do. You drooled at the prospect of all that extra money-spinning by capitalising on the death of one of our greatest ever musical treasures. You make me sick. She had a voice. People listened to her and worse still for some of your high and mighty mates the youth of our society *really* listened to her. She could have gotten them to do anything she wanted to just through the power of her song. Your bunch of charlatans felt threatened by her and they were terrified of her ability to influence people and that's why they gladly jumped on your bandwagon of death. Her lyrics inspired millions. More than any of your sick bunch of weirdos could ever do. You all like to think that you can control everyone and everything but inadvertently it was Phoenix who could control minds with ease because she had a natural talent and ability to do so, whereas you and your mob have to work so damn hard to contrive all of your attempts of control. So, you planned to kill her for your gain and for theirs."

"Look. She's dead now anyway. What does it matter?"

Judd shouted with rage. "It matters. Now if Satan was expecting someone to join him in Hell who am I to stand in his way?"

As the bullet entered Ocran le Boeuf's head the only thing that troubled Judd was whether he should have invested more time in torturing his victim instead of allowing him to die so quickly.

CHAPTER 42
THE ELEPHANT IN THE ROOM

"Well we didn't get to go to her funeral but it was a lovely memorial service," reflected Neima as she sank into Judd's sofa. Not quite ready to be alone after formally saying goodbye to Phoenix, the circle of friends had decided to return to Judd's Rotunda apartment for some much-needed companionship. Coming to terms with Phoenix's passing was still proving difficult for all of them.

"It was a lovely service, Neima," replied Brooke. "It was a nice send-off for a very special lady."

Mr. Mustard became excited jumping all over Judd as he always did when seeing him return to the apartment. "Down boy you'll ruin my suit." A few moments later, and only when Mr. Mustard believed that his welcoming ceremony had been deployed completely, did he comply with his owner's request and settle back under the dining table.

Judd removed his jacket and placed it on the back of the dining chair. He loosened his tie and made his way over to his drinks cabinet, pouring himself a whisky. "Anyone else?"

"I'd prefer a cup of tea if I'm being honest," said Neima.

"Me too," said Ben Francis.

"And me," said Crystal.

"Well, how very rock and roll of you all. Phoenix would never have approved." joked Judd.

"I'll pop the kettle on and make a pot," offered Brooke. For now, Brooke had moved into the Rotunda apartment as she and Judd contemplated what their next property move should be now that they were married. The apartment was ideal for a single man and his dog, and not too bad for a couple either, but it was not perfect when planning to start a family and Brooke liked to do a spot of gardening which the luxury apartment was unable to offer. Judd was still in the process of deciding whether to keep the apartment on however because it had been an ideal base for the PI business.

"I'll have a whisky with you, Judd."

"Coming right up Mr. Chamberlain."

"Can I have a coke please?"

"Of course you can, Xanthe. Yasmin? Sadie?"

"Tea," answered Sadie.

"Yeah, me too," concurred Yasmin.

Judd handed out his share of the drinks and then sat down. "To Phoenix," he said raising his glass.

"To Phoenix," said everyone else, with William and Xanthe being able to physically join in and raise their glasses to the deceased superstar.

Judd loosened his tie some more and pulled out the guitar pick necklace from beneath his shirt. "I shall treasure this for as long as I live," he said. "And the guitar that goes with it."

"She was one special lady," said Neima. "I'm disappointed that Ocran didn't show. He seems to have disappeared off the face of the earth."

"Just another of life's charlatans who can't be relied upon, Neima," said Judd, secretly knowing what the fate had been for Mr. Le Bouef.

Brooke walked in from the kitchen holding a tray. "Ok, I've made a nice strong pot. Here's some mugs, Judd's dining possessions don't stretch to a fine bone china tea service I'm afraid. Feel free to help yourself to milk and sugar."

"Why do I need a fine bone china tea service?" asked Judd.

"When you need to entertain several visitors," answered Brooke.

"Point taken."

"At least that scumbag Kaleb didn't outlive her long," said William.

"Yeah, that would have been a tad unfair if he had," agreed Judd.

An awkward silence fell for a few moments. Not everyone in the room was as comfortable as the two friends in wishing someone dead, even if it was a lowlife such as Kaleb.

"So, what happened, exactly?" asked Sadie.

"The official report is leaning towards accidental death or suicide," said Ben.

"Poetic justice in my book," said Judd.

"I have to agree," said Neima. "He was never any good for Phoenix."

"Pamela Courson," said Xanthe.

"What was that, Xanthe?" asked Judd.

"Pamela Courson. She was the girlfriend of Jim Morrison, the lead singer of the Doors who was pronounced dead at the age of 27 on July the third 1971. Jim was the last of four musicians to die between the years of 1969 and 1971 which provided great credence to the notion of a 27 club. The others being Brian Jones of the Rolling Stones, guitar wizard Jimi Hendrix and the husky-voiced Janis Joplin.

"Pamela Courson reportedly found Jim Morrison dead in a bathtub but as there was no autopsy, as in the case of

Phoenix, doubt is placed on his death. Pamela Courson, the girlfriend of Jim Morrison also died at the age of 27 as did Kaleb Rodriguez boyfriend of Phoenix Easter. Heroin was involved in her death and ironically, she was even born in a town called Weed in California. There are several parallels evident with Jim, Phoenix, Pamela and Kaleb."

"Xanthe has a way of presenting her words in a very matter-of-fact style. She is unable to dress them up with any tact and emotion but she means no harm" offered Ben Francis.

"It's ok," said Neima. "It's quite fascinating really, and besides there are parallels afoot, she's right about that. And she's correct that Phoenix didn't have an autopsy."

Xanthe continued. "Some theories suggest that as there was no autopsy performed on Jim Morrison that he could have faked his own death. He had become very disillusioned with the music business and in simple terms, he wanted out so he had to find a way to do so. I myself do not subscribe to the theory as Jim Morrison could not have lived a long and healthy life due to his intense approach to taking alcohol and drugs."

Inadvertently Xanthe had now firmly planted the seed in everyone's minds and in truth, each and every person present had at least considered that Phoenix could still be alive. Xanthe had simply exposed the elephant in the room.

Could Phoenix Easter really have faked her own death?

There were certainly a variety of mysterious things that surrounded her death and didn't quite add up. There had been no public funeral. There had not even been a private funeral which her most closest of allies had attended. There was no body available to exhume and the ashes that Gia Talia provided could actually have been ashes of anything. As already mentioned by Xanthe, there had been no autopsy and no post-mortem, even though this was the unexpected and potentially unnatural death of a 27-year-old high-profile celebrity.

Crystal broke into everyone's thoughts and brought people back into the room as they each reflected on their own take of the 'elephant'. "Judd, that guitar pick is lovely isn't it? May I take a closer look?"

"Yeah sure, but handle with care."

"Oh, I will, don't worry. I understand how precious it is to you."

Judd removed the chain from his neck and passed it to Crystal who held and cradled the guitar pick carefully. She began to study it quite intensely as the rest of the gathering moved on with their various topics of conversations. Then subconsciously Crystal began to drift away and became detached from the others in the room. Judd couldn't help but notice the smile appear on her face.

CHAPTER 43
THE MIRACLE OF BARGEMON?

Following the somewhat manic events of Las Vegas, Judd and Brooke had chosen a road trip across the South of France to be their second honeymoon. They had already enjoyed the more obvious locations of Monaco, St Tropez, Cannes and Nice, and were now heading further north into the medieval and lesser known villages of the Departement of the Var.

Taking the road from Callas, their next stop was to be Bargemon before settling in their final destination of Seillans.

Judd found himself feeling a little foolish as he steered the car along the ever-present bends of the road because he had, somewhat naively perhaps, hoped to bump into a certain somebody whilst in France. He had partly suggested the French Riviera to Brooke as a good honeymoon location for two personal ulterior reasons. The first, to catch a football match as Monaco hosted the team from Birmingham that he supported, and the second with the hope of somehow catching sight of an alive and kicking Phoenix Easter!

Always open to the concept of conspiracy theories, Judd had never been able to fully accept that Phoenix had died at the age of 27 and part of him had always suspected that Phoenix had faked her own death. He often reflected on the conversation that he had had with Phoenix when she had articulated her love for the South of France, and how in the same conversation she had suggested that perhaps she had reached her musical peak.

And what was it she had said in relation to the 27 club: "I won't join it by my own hand, Judd. *Not like they think anyway.*" After much thought, Judd now interpreted that remark to mean that she would join the club by her own doing but not by taking her own life.

And so, it made sense to Judd that Phoenix may have chosen to go out at the height of her fame, and if that exit was via very dramatic circumstances, such as death, then she would be forever 27 and forever a superstar. It was a theory he just couldn't shake from his soul since the world believed they had lost a much-loved singer-songwriter to the cursed 27 club.

Typically, Judd had researched and researched all the hypothesis and angles of the 27 club, becoming almost as knowledgeable as Xanthe, and he had discovered that on average brain activity decreases after the age of 27. Did Phoenix know this? Did she truly believe that she had peaked?

And after Crystal had cradled the guitar pick that Phoenix had gifted to him the psychic medium had taken him to one side and told him in no uncertain terms that the energies that she was retrieving from the object were from a person who was very much alive. However, they did discuss the possibility that Crystal could have been sensing the messages radiating from Phoenix's creative and musical energy that would inevitably live on as opposed to sensing the spirit of her living being. But by the same token Crystal had not felt the energies of someone who had passed either.

But of course, amongst all of those thousands of people amongst the crowds of the Cote D'Azur he had failed to spot Phoenix Easter.

Even if Judd's half-baked theory had been correct would she not have undergone plastic surgery in order to disguise herself from the world she had chosen to leave behind? Is it really that easy for someone as famous as Phoenix Easter to slip away from the phenomena that surrounds her in death as well as life?

Realising that Phoenix would have needed to secure a fake identity, being an ex-detective turned PI, Judd knew all too well that gaining a fake ID would not have been impossible for someone with Phoenix's status, especially if she had received help to disappear from the notorious Talias.

Judd also realised that with all his investigative skills and usual doggedness he could have researched Phoenix's death a lot more than he had done. He had deliberately chosen not to test the ashes in the urn which still stood in Neima's home. They had discussed him scattering them somewhere appropriate whilst he was in the South of France considering Phoenix had expressed her love for the place so much, but Neima still wasn't ready to give them up. Judd didn't believe that she ever would be. He had deliberately chosen not to track down and interrogate the names of those who had certified Phoenix to be dead. He had deliberately decided not to push his former colleagues in the police forensic department to check for Phoenix's DNA in Kaleb's bathroom. If all of this was what Phoenix wanted who was he to upset the apple cart. But that didn't thwart his curiosity regarding the death of the amazing young woman whom he had only had the privilege of knowing for a relatively short amount of time but nevertheless one whom he had considered to be a friend.

So, Judd had left the French Riviera behind not really all that surprised that he had failed to discover Phoenix to be alive and well. He was also on honeymoon and he had never been his intention to seriously investigate Phoenix's whereabouts in line with his usual work ethic, he had just kept one eye and his mind open to the hope of coming across her at some point. He had decided it best not to mention his theory to Brooke either. Primarily their honeymoon was about spending quality time together in spite of any ulterior motives.

As the road bent for the umpteenth time, Brooke spoke in that husky soft voice of hers. "Before we enter the village centre, Judd, we can stop off and fill our empty bottles at one of the natural water fountains. The first one we come across, according to the guidebook, depicts a statue of a lady holding a shell."

"Sounds good, I'm a little parched due to this gorgeous weather anyway. I believe Posh and Becks once had a place here, you know, in Bargemon."

"Really? Well that doesn't surprise me, it's not that far from the glitz and fashion status of St Tropez and Monaco should you need it, and both Mr. and Mrs. B no doubt would, yet it seems a far more tranquil setting for someone famous to slip away."

Brooke's words couldn't help but resonate with Judd. "Yeah, you're not wrong there are you, Brooke?"

"The travel guide describes Bargemon as a popular retreat for many renowned poets and artists."

"You don't say?" Now Judd's mind was doing ten to the dozen. "Musicians too I shouldn't wonder."

"Slow down here Judd, that opening just there must be the fountain we need."

Judd was able to pull into ample parking space at the side of the road. He and Brooke gathered the empty bottles and began to walk the 10 yards or so towards the ungated entrance. The heat hit them straight away as they stepped from the parked car. That was one reason why Judd took note of the figure that appeared from beneath the shade of the olive trees carrying her own bottle of recently filled spring water. She was covered from head to toe in linen clothing, including a headscarf. Ok, so it would be a material that was cool on the skin but it was clearly not a costume of religious significance so why wear so much clothing on such a hot day?

As the figure left the small entrance, she nearly bumped into an elderly gentleman who was ahead of Judd and Brooke, and that's when Judd noticed something very significant, just for a moment but it was long enough.

"Pardon, Monsieur," she said. The words had been said very quickly but Judd didn't believe they had been spoken by a native French tongue. Furthermore, the smile that had been generated for that spilt-second to accompany the apology revealed a gold tooth which sparkled in the sunlight contrasting the colour of the dark sunglasses that dominated the upper half of the face.

"It couldn't be. Could it?" Judd dared to imagine the impossible.

The figure hadn't even noticed Judd or Brooke and was moving away now towards the village centre. Even that swagger seemed familiar beneath the flapping linen. Judd almost called out the name 'Phoenix' but resisted just in case he was wrong. Plus, Brooke would have thought he'd turned crazy in the intense sun. She hadn't seemed to recognise the stranger as being Phoenix so perhaps Judd's mind had simply projected pre-conceived expectations on the female that had just passed before them. His hope of seeing Phoenix again had merely played a trick on his eyes.

Brooke led Judd down the three steps beneath the low hanging olive tree branches towards the fountain. The couple waited patiently for the elderly Frenchman to fill his bottle from the man-made brass tap that had been included at some point in the mouth of a weathered stone face that sat beneath the smiling lady holding a shell. The fountain sat in the middle of what could be described as a small courtyard, so Judd was able to walk beyond the fountain and marvel at the view of the forest covered hills that nestled amongst the terracotta rooftops of either the village of Claviers or Callas, he wasn't sure which.

However, in spite of this landscape of beauty before him, he couldn't shake the image of the lady with the gold tooth whom he had witnessed moments earlier.

Had it been Phoenix?

Bargemon, my God it even sounded a little like Birmingham thought Judd. Birmingham, the only other place that Phoenix would love to be, but she could never have pulled that one off following the faking of her own death. Or was Judd simply trying to make tenuous connections in the hope that Phoenix was alive that just weren't there?

By now the fountain had become vacant for Brooke to begin the process of filling the bottles. "Babe, while you're doing that I'm just going to run ahead and check out the layout of the village centre, just so we can use our time more productively."

"Ok, throw me the car keys, I'll stick these in the cool bag and follow you down. I think it's a small village so I should find you easy enough."

"Ok. Love you."

"I love you too."

Once out of sight from his wife, Judd put a distinct pace in his step hoping that he could catch up with the linen-clad lady with the gold tooth.

He was soon approaching the village centre and the two large trees that provided a significant amount of shade across the village. He just about caught sight of the figure turn the corner at the church and he broke into a jog.

Judd passed the central fountain which doubled up as perhaps the world's most attractive traffic island and he also passed through the communal area of seating and tables that were shared amongst the bars and restaurants. Those that were relaxing and enjoying their afternoon drinks were a little surprised to see someone in such a rush.

The church was an overwhelming structure. It seemed

out of scale with the rest of the village yet by the same token its size enabled it to blend in with the place, even producing a wall for the al-fresco dining area of one of the restaurants. Never a religious man by any stretch of the imagination, subconsciously stimulated by the huge church Judd found himself looking upwards to the cloudless blue sky for some kind of divine support and noticed the large spire with its set of weathered gargoyles. He turned the corner and Phoenix was nowhere to be seen. His only hope was that she had entered the church.

He passed the huge stone cross that was on the exterior wall and then passed through the two olive trees that sat in terracotta pots either side of the entrance, which typically already had the doors open for this particular church to welcome visitors

Once inside Judd could hear the sound of Gregorian chanting being played over the sound system. His trainers made no sound as they moved across the authentic black and grey tiled floor, and with each step, he was moving from bright sunshine to an environment of darkness and cooling shade. He was able to make out that someone was sitting at the front of the church. The figure was a little silhouetted but they seemed to be wearing a headscarf. Judd's stomach turned over and over. He was nervous beyond anything he had ever felt before. Was he really about to meet Phoenix Easter again after believing she was dead?

He moved past the statue of Litanie a Saint Michel Archange who had a sword and spear in respective hands and a slain dragon at his feet. The Englishman couldn't help but feel slightly confused, wasn't St George supposed to be the dragon slayer? Nevertheless, he didn't dwell on his confusion or self-recognised ignorance, he had far more pressing matters to attend to.

Judd continued slowly down the centre of the church. He spotted a statue of Christ to his left depicted in red and blue clothing and the painting of an intriguing female with blue eyes and long golden locks wearing a green dress hovering above the village in a majestic quality. Judd briefly wondered what her story could be and her striking features and comparison to Phoenix's golden dreads didn't escape him either. Judd was unable to read much of the French wording that accompanied the painting but he could decipher that the canvas depicted the lady representing an apparition or miracle appearing. Totally unknown to Judd, this church in Bargemon was recognised historically as a catalyst for miracles and pilgrimages have taken place here since the 1600s.

Was Judd about to witness another miracle here today?

Was Phoenix going to appear to him like a miracle?

Was she literally going to appear like a phoenix out of the flames?

He found the courage to sit behind the figure that still hadn't turned to acknowledge Judd's presence.

Judd gulped, a sound that echoed through the unique acoustics of the church. "Hello, Phoenix," he said nervously.

Finally, this was the prompt required for the figure to turn around and face Judd.

ABOUT THE AUTHOR

Martin Tracey is an author who likes to push the boundaries of reality. He lives in Birmingham, England and is married with two daughters. His passions include The Beatles and Wolverhampton Wanderers.

JUDD STONE WILL RETURN IN

Lunar

Printed in Poland
by Amazon Fulfillment
Poland Sp. z o.o., Wrocław